Angels Prostate Fall

OTHER BOOKS BY MARSHALL TERRY

Old Liberty
Tom Northway
Dallas Stories
Ringer
My Father's Hands
Land of Hope and Glory

Angels Prostate Fall

A Novel by

MARSHALL TERRY

SOUTHERN METHODIST
UNIVERSITY PRESS
Dallas

This novel is a work of fiction. Names, characters, places, and incidents are either the product of the author's imagination or are used fictitiously.

––––––––

Requests for permission to reproduce material from this work should be sent to:
Rights and Permissions
Southern Methodist University Press
PO Box 750415
Dallas, Texas 75275-0415

A portion of this novel was first published in *Southwest Review* (Spring-Summer 1995), has been anthologized in *Texas Bound, Book II: 22 Texas Stories,* and was included on the audiotape *Texas Bound III, 7 by 7: More Stories by Texas Writers, Read by Texas Actors.*

LIBRARY OF CONGRESS CATALOGING-IN-PUBLICATION DATA

Terry, Marshall, 1931–

    Angels prostate fall : a novel / by Marshall Terry.—1st ed.
      p. cm.
    ISBN 0-87074-463-1 (alk. paper)
    1. Prostate—Cancer—Patients—Fiction. 2. College teachers—Fiction. I. Title.

PS3570.E699 A86 2001
813'.54—dc21   2001032048

Jacket photograph "Act #9, 1994" by Nic Nicosia. Compliments of Nic Nicosia and Dunn and Brown Contemporary

Design by Tom Dawson

Printed in the United States of America on acid-free paper

10 9 8 7 6 5 4 3 2 1

To Toni, again and always

CHAPTER

1

ALL SPRING AND SUMMER Stanley Morris has gone around with odd old tunes in his head that no one else would think of or remember.

Now, in dog day August, it's "Twilight Time" that keeps threading through his mind.

"Heaven-ly da of da da da, it's—twi-light time . . ."

Doodle-de da da da . . . The Platters? The Coasters? The Drifters? Ink Spots? Sun Spots? The Plates? Saucers? The Forks? The Spoons?

Stanley lives near his university in a small community set between Dallas and Ft. Worth in the ever-burgeoning "Metroplex." He gets in his big old car and drives over to the complex of professional buildings by the hospital off the freeway. With the crazy traffic and drivers on the roads and highways along the way he would drive a semi cab if he could get away with it. He parks and goes into Building A to get his records from Dr. Fishbein so he can take them over to Dr. Miller in Building C.

Stanley's university is forcing the faculty to choose to give up their old doctors to go on a new medical plan with higher premiums and better coverage. Stanley's old friend and internist Dr. Witherspoon is threatening to retire anyway so he has referred him to young Dr. Whittle. Stanley's eye doctor, whom he has seen since the strange incident suffered in the mountains, is off the list anyway, so that leaves just the urological base not covered, so to speak. His old buddy Fishbein is off network too so Witherspoon has recommended Miller.

He has had a long, rich relationship with Fishbein, Stanley thinks as he goes into his office. Like twenty years. It's a shame to have to change. Stanley has called Fishbein jokingly "the Man with the Golden Finger." Actually the jolly little man has a finger of steel. Once, in the midst of a digital rectal exam Fishbein is moved to tell Stanley about his only son, Albert, who has flunked out of med school and is now in the submarine service. Stanley has been to see him just two months ago, so he has no worries on that score. "Smooth as a walnut!" Fishbein has barked at him in glee. "You sure don't have cancer!"

Da da da—da da da dah—la da de da . . .

"I called for my records in order that I can transfer them to Dr. Miller," he says to the young woman at the desk. She's a new one from two months ago. Fishbein always seems to have different people out front, as opposed to dear old Witherspoon, whose wife and nurse, who look so much alike they may be sisters, are always sitting in matched chairs smiling placidly at you.

"Mr. Stanley?" she says.

"Mr. Morris," Stanley says.

"Oh. Yeah. That's right. Morris."

"I believe it is."

So much for twenty years.

Humming the Platters or Coasters or Drifters ditty, he walks through the maze of halls and byways between Building A and Building C. He passes doctors and nurses and aides in white smocks and in green caps and smocks and patients moving slowly along the halls shaking, shambling, being helped, or rolled, shuffling with canes, on crutches, or like himself a month ago with patches or bandages on their eyes.

Dr. Miller's office, or the office he seems to share with Drs. Martz and Wu, is not bright and jolly like Fishbein's. It is stark, with just a print or two of hunting dogs and a somber tapestry on the walls. He hands the folder to the woman at the desk. She has very large eyes, like fish that swim in a bowl, behind her thick, magnified glasses. She looks startled to receive such an object as this folder.

"What can we do for you?" she says.

"Oh— Nothing. Right now, I mean. I called. You said—someone did—that you, actually that Dr. Miller, would accept me as a patient. I'm changing medical plans. I am newly on the Uni-Pro Coalition Network. OK?"

"Mr. Morris?"

"Right," he says. They seem to be able to read the name on a folder.

"Have a seat," she says. "Dr. Miller will want to see you."

"Thanks, but there's no need. I am just delivering the records."

"Have a seat," she says. "I'll tell him. He'll want to see you."

This sounds like an order. He sits.

In a little while she takes him into an examination room and asks for a urine sample.

"Really," he says. He did not come here today to be examined.

It's just been a couple of months. Smooth as a walnut. But he kind of has to go anyway, so he yields on the urine front. A nurse comes and nods at him and collects the cocktail. Then the door opens and a massive, not to say apelike, figure appears. It has a black beard and a thick neck and head and terribly penetrating black eyes and a white coat with *Dr. Miller* written on the pocket. He shifts his feet and seems about to leap up or sideways and holds out his hand.

Stanley takes it. This Miller has a small, strong hand.

"What can we do for you?" he says.

Stanley shrugs. He feels small and out of place, as if he is engaged in a bad joke. He knows he is fine. The last thing he desires or needs is an examination. "Nothing," he says to himself. "Not a thing. I was just passing by and thought I'd drop the folder off and behold you, and I must say you have surpassed my expectations."

"Not much," he answers. "I am just checking in, as a new patient. Thought I'd say howdy."

"Take off your pants and shorts," the doctor orders. "We'll see what's what."

"I just had the exam," Stanley says. "Not long ago. Dr. Fishbein—"

"You want to be my patient, I'll say what's what. Take 'em down," Miller says, black eyes glinting with a strange obsidian light, cutting to the chase. Stanley sees that he is not the tapestry. That is Martz or Wu. This one is the hunter.

"You bet," Stanley says.

Dutifully he resigns and aligns himself to what the comedians used to call "the fickle finger of fate."

This guy is gentler than Fishbein, anyway.

As Stanley turns around, reassembling himself, Miller pulls off the white prophylactic glove with a "pop." His dark doctor eyes hold Stanley.

"I think I felt something," he says.

Stanley stares at him.

This mountebank. Charlatan. Pretending to be a doctor! Jesus! This massive black-eyed demon or fool staring back at him. This incredible trickster. Jokesmith—

"Right on the left edge. Just a—tiny—rough spot."

"That is impossible," Stanley says, but only to himself. "You are wrong. Perhaps demented. You are a demented person, thank you very much, and I am putting on my trousers and buckling up my belt and leaving here in search of a sane doctor. Kidding around is OK, but—Jesus—"

"Miss Hish will make you an appointment for a biopsy," Dr. Miller says. "Then we'll take a look and see what's what."

He extends again his remarkable small, strong hand.

"Pleasure to meet you, sir," he says.

"Oh my," Stanley says.

Back home, air-conditioning thrumming in the old house, Stanley tells Olive he may have a little problem.

Her green eyes take on a shade of blue in concern.

"There are all kinds of reasons for a rough spot," he says. "The odds are heavily against it being malignant, or anything like that."

"Did he say so or are you saying so?" she says.

"I'm saying so," says Stanley. "It's ridiculous. The semester is about to begin. I have a full teaching load. I have committee duties. I'm supposed to make a talk to the new students. Housman one more time? I don't have time for foolishness. Art Baker had a biopsy, he said it hurts like hell. They shoot a needle into you. *Ka-ping!*"

"Would you like to be sinful and have a steak tonight?" she says. "A little wine?"

He nods. "And a little Scotch beforehand," he says.

"'Afore ye go,'" she says.

He shrugs. That's a little more levity than he wishes.

Dr. Miller does the biopsy in his office, with the help of a bland man called Johnny who runs the machine. He laughs that he should be called "Dick" instead of Johnny. "Moby Dick the harpoon guy," he says. Ha ha.

"Moby Dick was the whale, not the harpoon guy," Stanley says. "That was Queequeg."

"Oh no, I wouldn't want to be called that," says Johnny, hands caressing the dials and screens on his smooth machine.

Dr. Miller swings in and without a word hurls six consecutive harpoons through Stanley into his target chestnut. Each arrives with a delicious little blossom of pain.

"I'll call you in four days," the doctor says.

"That wasn't bad, was it?" Johnny says.

"How does it work exactly?" says Stanley.

"The needle goes in, makes the hit, and takes a core that comes back out through the needle for the lab. Pretty slick, eh? Couldn't do it this easy just a couple of years ago."

"Hurray for technology," Stanley says, though he feels ambivalent.

All week long, as the campus gears up to begin the term, Stanley

goes around consciously humming upbeat old tunes like "Yankee
Doodle Dandy" and "Pack Up Your Troubles in Your Old Kit Bag"
while "Twilight Time" keeps oozing up from his subconscious.

The earnest chaplain, Andy Hall, encounters him on campus
and takes Stanley's lapel and leans to confide to him. "You remember Jack Bompers?" he asks. "He went on to Virginia?"

"Do I remember him?" Stanley says. "He just left last year, he
was our dean, for Christ's sake."

"Has prostate cancer," the chaplain says. "Just found out. Going
to have a prostatectomy. I talked with him by phone last night. He
is sore afraid, but he is coming to terms with his mortality."

"I am very glad," says Stanley.

There are a dozen reasons you can have a rough spot, just a tiny
spot, on your chestnut, he thinks. (He has come to think of it as his
chestnut since he saw the big color picture of the male and his parts
on the wall in Dr. Miller's examination room: the prostate there
being characterized as the size of a chestnut. Seeing the picture worried Stanley. The chestnut was up there right in the middle of things,
it looked pretty inaccessible, and wired up to all the rest.)

Why in the hell didn't Fishbein find it, feel the little rough spot?
No wonder he had gotten to be so jolly, he was getting senile. But
Stanley had liked old Fishbein. Every time he'd taken him a book or
an article—for Fishbein was a reader and a thinker of sorts—the
jolly fellow would stick his head out into the hallway and yell up to
the desk, "This one's on the house for Stanley!" You had to love old
Fishbein.

In five days the doctor's office calls, Stanley wondering if they
had forgotten or lost the cores or what, to say the pathologists in
Dallas can't tell, they disagree over one of the cores, the one right at

the left edge that Miller had felt. Can't tell if it's malignant or not. They are sending it on to Mayo, it will be a few days more.

"They're sending it to Dr. Flimflam, or whatever his name is, the nation's most respected and famous and expert pathologist."

"Hey, don't you feel special?" Olive says. "But, really, doesn't that make you feel like it probably isn't?" Isn't cancer, she means, not even wishing to say the word. Her eyes are kind, but there's a lot of that worried blue in them.

Stanley rolls his own brown eyes, one good, one bad. He would like for it to sound encouraging but somehow it really doesn't. It just sounds even more ridiculous, that in this city full of pathologists and labs and medical expertise they have to send his prostate sample to the Mayo Clinic.

Another three days go by and he is still bleeding a little from the Moby Dicking.

When the call finally comes the nurse says Dr. Miller himself will speak to him.

"It's a malignancy," he says. "Just that one spot. The good news is that it appears to be contained, though we can't be sure it hasn't spread outside the prostate. The bad news, of course, is that you have cancer. It's a Gleason's Five."

Involuntarily Stanley laughs, seeing Jackie Gleason in his mind. Have they named prostate cancers after Jackie Gleason?

"What? Is something funny?" Miller asks.

"Gleason's what?"

"Five. Meaning a mid-level malignancy. Not way up there but requiring attention. Yes?"

Yes. Oh yes.

Dr. Miller suggests he come in and talk about it, the alternatives, which seem to be leave it alone, take it out or radiate it. He'll send some information. Stanley says he'll be there, with Mrs. Morris.

Dr. Miller's private office, as opposed to his stark reception area and sterile examination rooms, is pleasant. Homey. He seems a different man in here. A person.

Prints of retrieving dogs are on the wall. Hunting and fishing magazines are on the coffee table. Stanley's wingback chair is slip-covered in a pattern of muted colors. Olive sits on a chair beside him. Dr. Lester Miller sits behind his desk wearing small round glasses intensifying the penetrating gaze of his dark eyes. He rolls a Mont Blanc pen in his small hands.

They talk about it.

It's really pretty simple, Stanley gathers from what he says. If you're fifty or sixty and in good shape, go for the fence, go for the cure. If you're seventy, radiate. Some younger men choose to radiate anyway. It can be as effective. If you're eighty, smile and be glad you just got it, right? It's probably not going to kill you sooner than anything else. Every man gets cancer of the prostate sooner or later.

There are hazards to the surgery or to radiation, the doctor proceeds to explain. It's a tricky little operation. Slit you from the belly to the groin. First, you get the lymph nodes in the stomach. If they're OK, go on. Delicado. Take a lot of stuff apart and put it back together. Bleeding is a possibility, so you give two units of your own blood before. God! Suddenly Stanley thinks of Jim Anderson, the anthropologist. Then, if it hasn't spread outside the prostate you can

save the veins, maybe avoid impotence. Later, after a successful removal, there can be bad, degrading urinary problems.

"I suppose you have a good success rate with this operation?"
Olive says.

The doctor nods, up and down but crossways too. He's honest,
not willing to claim perfection. He does it almost every morning, this
operation. He always operates with his partner, Dr. Martz. No urological surgeon would ever operate alone.

Reassuring, eh?

So?

"I think I want to go ahead and have it out," says Stanley.

"Think about it," Miller says. But he smiles and nods. This is a
good man. His smile is warm and wonderful, really reassuring. Go
for it, Stanley, babe, it says. How could Stanley have thought he
looked apelike? Actually, he resembles Moses.

And now, through the absurdity of it, the feeling that you are
witnessing something happening to someone else, Stanley is vaguely
glad he wandered in here with his file from old Fishbein.

"I don't think he's all that stern, or forbidding," Olive says, im-
pressed with Dr. Miller. "I think he's very human and answers
straight. Professional. Careful to let you know what's what. He spent
a lot of time with us."

Da da dah, da da da dah, Stanley hums.

He goes to see his old buddy Doc Witherspoon, the retiring internist. The old doc has toy soldiers on his shelves and desk. Dragoons and lancers and marching Scots in kilts. He is a homeopath by
nature, basically against surgery.

"You're in good shape. You can stand it. But it's a damn trau-
matic operation, Stanley. You know—I've got some literature here."

He thrashes around and comes up with an article in a medical journal.

"There's good opinion that says just leave it alone. Keep checking it. There are odds it may just stay the way it is."

That might make you a little nervous, Stanley thinks. He has made up his mind.

He gets his affairs in order. He tells his department chairman, a few others. He makes a day-to-day schedule of his teaching and other obligations. He speaks to the incoming students, transfers but mostly freshpersons, on A. E. Housman's *Introductory Lecture.* The only pleasure that does not diminish with fulfillment is learning. "Other desires perish in their gratification, but the desire of knowledge never." He believes this. It goes by them, or over them. In the midst of leaving home and beginning college, in their vitality and gleaming youth, they do not in this moment seem to comprehend this message, or care. In time to come, he thinks, they will.

He talks to Dr. Miller again. Ten years ago, this friend of his, Jim Anderson, died during this same operation, bled to death on the operating table. Miller looks at him darkly. "We have improved our techniques greatly in the last decade," he rejoins. "But do not ever think I said it is not serious and has no risk."

The operation is set for September 16. Stanley sees in his pocket diary that this is the date of Rosh Hashanah. He thinks of his brother in the East, who has just had his foot removed because of diabetes. Old Barry will think he's trying to upstage him. He asks his grad student Joe Green to take over his writing section while he's out. Joe says he will, though he is just hanging in there himself, he may leave school and go back to playing music in New Orleans or L.A. This worries Stanley. Surely Joe is meant to be a teacher. Stanley pays all his bills and prenotifies the medical plan of the operation. He goes to the bank with a signature card so that Olive can get into the strongbox should the worst occur and he expire. He knows in his heart that he will live forever but he prepares.

In the blood donor substation in the shopping center Stanley has an eleven o'clock appointment to give blood for himself. He will need to give twice. It's crowded. The woman volunteer at the desk says it'll be a wait of an hour or more. He sits to wait.

An old man starts yelling at a nurse. "I think you are too old to give," she says.

"I'm only eighty-one," he yells.

They take him back to wherever it is you give, and in a while they wheel him back out. He has collapsed.

"I told him!" says his wife.

"Mr. Stanley," the woman at the desk calls out.

"Mr. Morris," he says. "Stanley Morris. Just like it says on the form."

A short fellow in a white smock that says *Claude, Blood Specialist* on the front comes shuffling up to the desk. He takes the form with a palsied hand, so the form shakes. He looks at Stanley with an askew, bloodshot eye.

"Mor-ris?" he says. "Morris? That your name? Morris?"

"Yes," Stanley says.

The man, Claude, starts spasming along his right side, his arm and shoulder jerk. He slams the form down on the desk.

"Ain't you got no middle initial?" he demands.

"What?" Stanley thinks the poor fellow must be demented. Must have had a stroke. Doing the best he can. "Oh, yes," he says. "I do. 'N.'"

"'N'?"

"Yes, sir. 'N.'"

"'N'? 'N'?" The man twitches and shakes convulsively. He hands Stanley a ballpoint from his pocket in a quivering hand. "All right! Slide that 'N' right in there—"

Stanley bends and slides the 'N' in between the *Stanley* and the *Morris* on the form.

"All right," the man says as a convulsion turns him around and he shuffles, or half topples, into the doorway of the room beyond.

Stanley hears him fall in there. The nurse runs in. They get him on a stretcher. Stanley stands against the wall. The ambulance comes. They take the man, Claude, away. "We're closing now. No more blood today," the woman says.

They close and lock the door.

"God," he says to Olive. "I thought he'd had a stroke. Dear God, he was having a stroke! And I just stood there. I thought he was demented. While all the time he was doing his duty to the end . . ."

"Don't feel guilty. What could you have done? That's terrible."

But he feels guilty.

"Oh yes—Claude. We buried Claude on Wednesday," says a new woman at the desk when he goes back a few days later to try to give again. "We'll miss Claude. He'd been here a long time, they tell me."

He goes to have a CAT scan to see if it, the malignancy, has spread.

Never having been scanned before—never having been in a

hospital since his appendix was removed at fourteen—Stanley is taken unawares. The portly woman in greens tells him to jump into this contraption and lie down. It is a rectangular machine. He takes his shoes off and hops in. Immediately she starts it up and tells him it will take half an hour. "Don't move at all," she says, "or it will have to be done all over again."

He is lying on his back. The machine comes down an inch or so from his nose. He panics, almost screams. Let me out of here! He can't breathe. He has not known what would happen. He has not composed himself. He needs to crack his arthritic wrist. His head is not on his neck right. He itches. His foot itches, his face itches, his ear itches. His balls itch. He is in a coffin that grinds and moves above and around him. He really is going to scream for them to stop it. He can't lie still in here. He is suffocating. He gasps—

He tries to say the Lord's Prayer but can't remember it. It comes to him disjoint, the pleas seem to have no coherence. The twilight ditty comes floating in, but he can't breathe. He tries to think of poetry. His grandfather could recite Gray's *Elegy in a Country Churchyard* through. "Buffalo Bill's defunct—" No, that won't do. "Apeneck Sweeney—" Yes. "Mrs. Porter and her daughter—" "Stately, plump Buck Mulli—" Ah. Ah, hell. An old horror movie, as the mechanism rolls so slowly from the head, so slowly, to the feet, and turns and comes grinding back at you again. Poe. Buried alive. Living death . . .

Finally it stops. He staggers up.

All weekend he is numb, waiting for the result.

It's OK. It hasn't spread to the bones. It's in the chestnut, and we are going to get it.

His daughter and her husband call from New York. Martin's parents are both doctors. All his uncles are doctors. The advice of these experts is don't do the knife, go with cryosurgery. Freeze it. It's the best and coolest method. Freeze that chestnut.

"Freeze it?" Stanley says. "Freeze it? What happens when it thaws?"

On the evening before the operation, drinking the gallon of Golitely, on and off the toilet, Stanley stops himself from entering his study and writing on his desk pad, "It's been wonderful."

He goes out into the big backyard where every spring he plants a garden of tomatoes, squash, cucumbers, beans, and seven kinds of peppers. There used to be, years ago, a colony of bees in the wall of his old house by the chimney. They had to take off the side of the house to get more than a hundred pounds of blackened honey out after an old man came and led the bees away. And still bees love this house, this yard, this place. Every spring, for a day or two, hundreds come down the chimney and lie on the rugs in the living room and den and just quietly lie there and die, and Stanley gently sweeps them up. Now a new hive has come and settled in the honeysuckle on the back of the old garage near where he plants his garden. They fly around his head in slow circles as he digs and waters, picks and prunes. Olive worries about their returning like this. She has visions of their cousins the African killer bees slowly making their way up here from Mexico.

What should he do? Try to get rid of them? Poison the bees? When it gets cold, he'll take the honeysuckle off the back of the garage, and see if—

See if.

In the black early morning, cleaned out and clear as a bell, he goes with Olive and is admitted to the hospital.

He chats with the anesthesiologist, to whom he has lied, saying he has no history of breathing difficulty whereas all through childhood he had asthma. Let's just do it, right? She gives him a little something and says she'll be right here by him.

Drs. Miller and Martz greet him. The old tune now in his mind is a hymn, an oddly humorous hymn. "All hail the power of Jesus' name—Let angels—" Nice play on words, eh? Prostrate/prostate. Ha. Martz is larger than Miller. His eyes are kind. They wear masks.

"What faith do you have?" Stanley thinks he asks them.

"Jewish," they say.

Yes. On Rosh Hashanah. What a good conjunction. Stanley smiles up at them, their strong, quick, white-sheathed hands. A new beginning. In a book by a former student on Jewish holy days he has found the prayer they pray this day. He has it in his mind. It is a prayer for healing and for mercy. Drifting off, Stanley, forcing his eyes to open, looks up and thinks he says the prayer to them, to the doctors.

He does not know if they hear the prayer.

CHAPTER

2

IN THE LONG FLOW of waking from the anesthesia, Stanley dreams and remembers. The visions come to him so vividly—not so much of his father whose passing was so far back in time but images of his mother, Flo, and the Colonel and Mack—dear God, Mack—that he is not sure whether their spirits are coming back to him or he is joining them.

Mack, Mack Williams, is his best friend since they were kids and briefly then his half-brother. Mack is a lawyer in this city now and has come out to the Highland U. campus to have lunch with Stanley. They are sitting in the Faculty Club when Mack looks up from his ravioli at him and gives him that old signature smile and wink. Mack has been a winker all his life. He holds the smile a moment too long, his brown eyes are sad. Stanley senses Mack's torment deep inside. Stanley has requested a private room in the club for them upstairs, hoping Mack will talk. Mack has been divorced, is living alone in a small apartment, is depressed.

Eight years ago, newly remarried, he greeted Stanley, with a sweep of his arm, at the doorway of the large new house he'd built way out on the city's northern perimeter.

"Doesn't it remind you of where we grew up?" he said, pointing across the drainage ditch, a clumpy field of prairie grass. One new wispy tree with feathery leaves stood bravely in the yard.

"Yes. Oh yes," Stanley lied.

They had grown up by woods, with stands of trees, and hills, and rich grass and soil, creeks flowing through, roaming as boys along paths on which Iroquois and Shawnee braves used to glide.

"Yes," Stanley said, nodding to the ditch with its bit of tainted water, the scraggly field, the thin lone tree.

Now Mack looks at him as if he's never seen him before and puts down the fork and piece of bread in his hands and holds them out in front of him over the table between them as if cradling something fragile, delicate. His hair is jet black still, his mouth thin, his face yet lean but lined, dark and ruddy, red-spotted at the cheeks, impassive. When Stanley and Mack were growing up the old gang used to call Mack the Great Stone Face when he was in one of his dark, inward moods; he would go smoldering and silent for days before he would snap out of it and in a surge lead them on some manic quest or caper.

"I sat up almost all night holding my old revolver, you know, the .38, my favorite one, the one you and I shot targets with right after I got out of the Marine Corps. God, was that more than thirty years ago?"

Stanley does not know guns, not really. He had a .22 rifle when he was a boy. In his closet he has now, in leather cases, relics, artifacts, an old Savage 30.06 rifle from his father and an old barrel-scrolled Baker shotgun from his father's father. He looks straight at Mack, who smiles, winks again. It chills Stanley. He does not wish to believe, to countenance, this. In Mack's face he sees the outline of Mack's mother's face, her manic smile, her slyness. He does not want to hear, almost pretends he doesn't. The terrible thing is, he can picture Mack sitting in his apartment holding the blue-black pistol, rotating it in his hands, clicking the loaded chamber, weighing its heft, contemplating the barrel's muzzle.

"Surely not," he says, trying to smile back.

Mack shrugs, picks up his fork, lifts a piece of ravioli, puts it back.

"You wouldn't ever do that, Mack," Stanley says. "Tell me that you wouldn't. Hey, I mean, Jesus, you—I—we love life too much. I mean, whatever— Think of all the things we've lived through, and over."

"Yeah. Just kidding. Sorry," Mack says. "Say, did I tell you I met a new woman at church?"

"What church? I mean, that's great—"

"Unitarian. They do our old Robert Frost poems, a little Emerson, secular benedictions. Named Martha. Good old-fashioned name, eh? She's a nice person. Her husband left her, years ago, with this kid. . . . Hell, she's nearly my own age. Do you think I'm facing reality?"

"Doubtless."

Mack's last wife was fifteen years his junior. Adored him, until she discovered he was not functioning in his profession, in society, in this world. Mack always the leader, Mack of the old American virtues, Mack the husband, father, lover, Mack the ever restless, never satisfied: Mack who should be at the top now, secure, respected, safe even from his own damn demons.

"But it may, yet, be early to—to get involved one more time, Mack, old Mack," Stanley almost says, but doesn't. What is Mack supposed to do, sit night after night in his apartment reading Michener?

Guns. Jesus, guns!

Stanley has thought Mack got away from guns. Mack always had loved them and had at least a dozen, but in his new house, with Marian and his two bluetick hounds, Pa and Pup, the guns had been relegated to a glass-front cabinet, more a collection than an arsenal. In the house before, with Hannah, Mack had them strategically placed. After all, they lived on a busy through street, a thoroughfare.

Going in Mack's house then, Stanley came to know there was a gun in a drawer of the chest in the entryway. Behind some Robert Service and Kipling in the bookshelf in the den room was a .357 Magnum. In the hall closet, on a nook concealed to the side, was an ugly short hard plastic pump shotgun. Guns were placed adroitly here and there, in the bedroom, kitchen, in the utility room over the jamb of the door to the connected garage. It had scared Stanley.

Going downstairs in the Faculty Club after their mostly uneaten lunch, Stanley is startled when Mack veers from their path to the door and approaches the Curmudgeons' Table with a jolly grin on his face and hand outstretched.

This is the long corner table where the Idealists, pessimists, Stoics, Cynics, and miscreants of the university sit at lunch and carve up the despicable administration, the hopeless student body, and

the terrible trustees, deploring in chorus the folly of higher education as practiced in America, the hegemony of sports, and the absurdity of life. It is Stanley's university's own little floating island, its
Laputa. At the table sit Pantagruel, Quixote, Heep, La Pasionara,
and Dr. Pangloss. Now manic, Mack approaches them in seeming
glee.

"What say?" he says, in the patois of the time of their growing
up. "What's going on? How are you men? I'm Mack Williams,
Stanley here's buddy. What say? What d'ya say? You guys all professors? Aren't you afraid to sit all together like that?"

Inder Singh, a chemist, rises to his slight but imperial height at
the head of the table. He does not offer his hand but bows.

"Doctor Singh," he says.

Mack beams. "Nice to meet you, Doc." Inder looks shocked to
be shaking Mack's strong hand. "Are you Indian? Look like a Pun-
jabi to me. They are proud, strong devils, like Texans. Right?" Mack
says, imparting some of the wisdom he has stored from Michener
and other purveyors of popular lore and history.

"I am Sikh," says Singh.

"Hey! You guys are something else, about the toughest and the
smartest, aren't you?"

Inder Singh's large eyes gleam. He bows again. "Yes," he says.
"Also, I am indeed from Punjab."

He looks at Stanley with new respect in light of his having such
an insightful friend as Mack.

"Beltrán-Luna." Professor Francisco Beltrán-Luna, a renowned
and somewhat crazy research scientist of national reputation, rises
and extends his hand. "I am, originally, from Panama."

Stanley looks to see if Ho Chi Bell will rise to claim his nationality and identity, but Ho Chi sits and looks sadly at his black bean soup as if it were a universe in itself. Ho Chi is a poet.

Beltrán-Luna is asking how Mack knows Stanley.

"He almost never sits with us, Professor Stanley," Singh says, "as he is a toady to the dean."

"Morris," Stanley says. "We do not at present have a dean."

"When we acquire another useless appendage of a dean, you will be a toady to him," Inder says.

Mack smiles sideways at this pleasantry. He is involved in telling Beltrán-Luna that he and Stanley grew up together, went off to college together, joined the Marine Corps reserve together, but Stanley stayed in college as he, Mack, went off to war.

"Or to her," interjects Eugenia Nott-Glass, a noted anthropologist, raising the option that the new dean may be a woman.

"Not likely," mutters Oakley Baum, a massive, one-eyed historian.

"Oh, so you have fought for your country, the terrible imperialist nation I deplore," exclaims Beltrán-Luna.

"He was a hero," Stanley says.

Old Mack served in the Mediterranean as a sergeant in a Marine color guard cruising around all the posh ports. He sent Stanley from one of them a "Great Golden Horny Bird," which was an erect penis and scrotum, the size of your hand and wingéd, cast in bronze. Stanley seems to have lost the damn thing somehow through the years, or perhaps Olive has thrown it away.

"I too fought for my country—my true country. I was involved in the fighting, at least, when the Yankees came again into Panama!

I was, at least, in the street, and caught in crossfire. Come, I will show you."

Beltrán-Luna takes Mack by the arm and pulls him off towards the Gentlemen's Room.

Singh sits. Stanley pulls up a chair by him and sits and looks pleasantly around the table. You never can do anything when Mack is on a high but sit by and catch him before he explodes.

"Of what race and descent is your friend, this Mack?" says Singh.

"Williams," Stanley says. "Very Welsh."

"That is a strong and rebellious, troubled race," says Singh.

"Yes. He likes to tell a story about when he stayed awhile in Wales. He would go to the post office to get his mail, and every time he went in the postmaster would say, 'What Williams?' going down the long list of all the Williamses until he came to 'Williams, Mack.' Would do it every morning."

Singh looks at Stanley as if he is a moron.

"There were so many, you see," Stanley says. "Almost the whole town was named Williams."

Francisco Beltrán-Luna and Mack come arm in arm out of the Gentlemen's Room. With his other hand Francisco, beaming, is stuffing his shirt back in his pants.

"Oh my," sighs Nott-Glass, making a mental note of this male behavior.

"Nice to meet you fellas," Mack says, his spasm of energy ebbing. "You all take good care of Stan the Man here. Let's go, Stanley."

"Hell of a guy," Mack says in the car. Smiles weakly at Stanley. "Showed me the scars all around his back and stomach where the machine-gun bullets ripped him. Lucky to have made it. What's he do? Something great?"

"Yes," says Stanley. For he does, actually. "He's been a leading researcher on DNA."

"Identity," Mack says.

"Look," says Stanley to his oldest friend, his best friend growing up, his spiritual brother now in fact his brother since Mack's father, the dear old fellow, married Stanley's mother, bless her lovely, wracked, departed bones.

"Look here, Mack, do take your medicine."

Mack looks at him darkly.

"I've been reading about it," he says, the red points deepening on his dark cheeks. "They say that shit makes you suicidal."

The next week Stanley is at his desk in his office marking student papers when he feels a presence. He looks up to see Milton Hooser, Mack's devoted young associate and partner in Mack's firm, standing before him. An arc of sunlight comes through the window at Stanley's left shoulder, seeming to emanate from the tops of tall buildings beyond the campus whose gleam and glitter extend now many miles all the way to Dallas. Glancing eastward, Stanley almost thinks he can see the faces of people in windows of those buildings. He thinks of the old poet who taught him and Mack in what was then called their freshman year in college, before the Korean Crisis, and the Marine reserve, who said how precisely one's "poet's eye" can see in the heightened moments of one's experience.

"It's Mack," says Milton Hooser, a tall young man in a dark undertaker's suit, as if he were dressed for the occasion.

Just beholding him there, his materialization before him, Stanley knows what he is going to say.

"Last night, I guess. Or early this morning," Milton says. "The police removed the body, and called me. I thought you would want to go to the apartment with me. I mean, you're the executor."

"Yes," Stanley says, strangely calm. "Of course."

He takes off his glasses. Rubs his eyes. Everything blurs through the window down the vista of the campus on to the skyscrapers of the city. He cannot even distinctly see the spire of the chapel just beyond. He readjusts his glasses and looks at the student's paper. He'd written his comments on it, hanging in his mind between a B+ and an A-. He puts the paper aside, in fairness not marking it, gets up and shakes Hooser's hand and pats his grieving shoulder, Mack as much a teacher as is Stanley, this his last disciple, and goes with him out of his Greek-columned building and to his car.

The small apartment has a tiny kitchen and dining nook, a bathroom, a room with books and television and travel magazines. Stanley sees his own slim book on Emerson placed on the shelf of books by the Frost, the Michener, the McMurtry, the Le Carré and the Deighton and the Casey. He sees the rifles and shotguns locked within the glass-front case.

The police inform him that Mack shot himself in the head with his favorite old .38 about 3:30 A.M. on the narrow single bed in the small bedroom. He left a short note on a yellow legal tablet which they confiscated and will release later.

In the bedroom Milton Hooser looks at the bed and says, "Oh, Jesus."

The bedclothes are soaked in blood.

When Stanley carefully pulls the comforter and sheet and pad off the bed and rolls them up, the mattress is also stained with caked blood from Mack's head.

Milton takes the pile of bedclothes from Stanley and goes out of the apartment building to the dumpster behind. Stanley looks at the clock by the bed, at Mack's gold-faced wristwatch lying there. A ballpoint also sits there. He bends and opens the top drawer of the bedside table. Things roll around inside. The drawer is full of bullets and goldfoil-wrapped condoms. Stanley shuts it.

"Are the kids coming here?" he says to Milton.

Mack's grown son and daughters are flying in.

"We're meeting them at the office. Then they'll come here."

"Well."

He picks up one end of the blood-crusted mattress. Milton takes the other end. Like automatons they carry the thing outside to the dumpster and cram it in on top of the bedclothes.

"Do you want to look around the apartment some more?"

"No."

He will come with the kids and help sort Mack's possessions out and pack them up.

Milton closes and locks the apartment door.

It is a drab apartment complex that sits out on the flat land in far north Dallas on the way to Oklahoma.

In Mack's office Stanley sits in Mack's chair for a moment at Mack's desk. He looks at the old chest of drawers in arm's reach that has been in Mack's family since pre–Civil War. It comes from Galena, Illinois, where the Williamses were in the furniture-making business in an establishment next to the Grants, who worked in leather. Stanley, the old Shawnee, looks at the message Mack, the

Iroquois, has left him on his desk: to his left a thick folder of debts; to the right, a slim folder of assets, mostly life insurance policies to the kids taken out so long ago that his suicide would not keep them from being paid.

Stanley gets up and walks backward from the desk. He thinks with sympathy of the new woman Mack has met, undoubtedly has romanced. She will be shocked.

When the daughters and son arrive they are children again. Stanley feels terribly old and burdened before them. He feels he should be clad in robes.

"Daddy was depressed," the daughters say. "Isn't there a note?"

Eyes brimming, the son says, "It was his conscious choice. He knew what he was doing. It was a very brave thing to do—a courageous act—wasn't it, Uncle Stanley?"

Stanley looks back at him. He tries to think about it truly, his memory spinning through and under the blanket of the anesthesia, his conscious and unconscious parts blending so he feels, his mind and memory revolving, a sense of peace and of whirling through his being, feels that he floats like the butterfly, is being stung by the bee. But now, even in the whirl he knows strongly that he, Stanley Morris, in any physical state or mental state, would want to go on living: wants to live, never to cease knowing, never to die.

Yes: in that sense, terribly courageous.

"Yes," he says to the grown, trembling son. "It was very brave."

Oh, Mack!

CHAPTER

3

THE COLONEL WAS A sergeant in World War I and a colonel in World War II. He was Mack's dad, and when Mack's mother died the Colonel called Stanley's mother and said, "Flo, would you like to get married?" and she jumped up and took off her back brace and her neck brace and put on her makeup and they did. The Colonel was eighty by then and Stanley's mother just seventy-three so he would go around with a goofy grin on his face calling her "my child bride."

That was—how many—years ago? He wonders, his mind floating under the anesthesia, his memory spinning like the colored lights revolving from the ceiling of the gym as the dancers shuffled around the floor at their high school prom. What were the names of those girls, who were their dates? How many years ago, he wonders, his consciousness floating, was it that his mother and the Colonel married? And how many years behind that—so many years—his time of "growing up"?

He sees them at the wedding in Mack's living room. His mother, Flo, wears a bright blue suit and pearls. The Colonel looks pretty dapper, for him, in a green jacket and blue tie and brown trousers and loafers and his service decoration in his lapel and his goofy, so-good-hearted gentle smile. The Colonel—he likes for Stanley and his sons to call him that—is a tough knot out of which has come the piece of oak that is his son Mack. The Colonel's name is Bert. He drove Mack and Stanley on their very first date when they were fourteen before they could legally drive in his green Pontiac with the Chief emblem on the hood. He embarrassed them by telling their dates, oh yes, Ann and Debbie were their names, corny jokes. Mack was so embarrassed he clammed up and would not speak to his date, Debbie, a stocky girl with many teeth, so pleasant, who even tried to laugh at the old jokes. Stanley's date was Ann. She was about a head taller than Stanley and quiet, a bit hunched over in her formal gown but very sweet and not begrudging Stanley's current lack of height. Like Stanley's father, the Colonel always kept a large garden when the boys were growing up, and in addition kept goats. He would give long, boring, detailed homilies on the healthful properties of the milk of goats. If he had had chin whiskers the Colonel would have at last resembled a venerable goat. Stanley has come to think, with the Colonel's anguish over his bipolar wife Miranda and all of Flo's constant friendship and care and concern for her, that Mack's father through the decades must have come to feel affection and even love for Stanley's mother years before they married.

"She listens to my stories," he would say after he and Flo were married, "and pretends she hasn't heard them all before."

Flo would smile at him lovingly.

Stanley can't remember any of the Colonel's corny old jokes that used to embarrass them. He tries, but all he remembers of that time is being so young and praying that he would grow up and maybe even achieve some height and be able to drive himself on dates in a smoother car than an old green Pontiac and later become a grown man and never tell corny jokes that would embarrass his children.

At the dance when Ann smiles down at him and Debbie smiles up at the silent Mack, all the colored lights, red and blue and green, from the revolving ball above them in the gym bounce down off these nice girls' teeth. The band plays "Stardust" and "Tenderly" and finally "Good Night, Sweetheart" and Debbie asks Mack if "Tenderly" can be their song, and Ann and Stanley agree that "Stardust" will be their song, and these are everybody's songs, and the Colonel drives them home and only cracks another terrible joke on their way home and waits patiently for each of them to take his girl to her front door.

Stanley would like to ask Mack what the old jokes were. Mack would remember them.

When Mack's mother died Stanley put on his dark pinstriped suit and flew down to Corpus Christi on the Gulf and rented a car and drove to Calm Harbor for her funeral. The minister, who did not know her, said how great her faith was, how she had been called to meet her Savior. Stanley expected Mack's mother to rattle the coffin in protest. She was an agnostic, a rationalist, who always encouraged Mack and his brother to be skeptical of orthodox religion, to be skeptical of Jesus, one of whose sheep she definitely was not.

Stanley's dark pinstripe suit is too heavy for the spring afternoon and evening at Calm Harbor. It is humid. Rain clouds hover over the Colonel's house and dock. The boats tied along the slip leading out to the bay bounce on the windy waves. It is squalling out over the gray and choppy coastal sea. He drinks Scotch whiskey and takes off the suit coat and tries to have a wake with the Colonel and Mack and Mack's brother Mort, but they are terribly serious and drink without smiling or telling stories, a dour Welsh lot, in their grief. Stanley puts his glass down and his coat back on and drives over to the coastal city and flies home.

By the time he arrives home the Colonel is already on the phone to Flo, asking her to marry him.

Always when Stanley goes down to the water to visit them at Calm Harbor the Colonel flies his fish flag in his honor.

Always when he is there Stanley feels like a boy. His mother tells him to speak up and not to mumble, meaning to speak loud enough for her and Bert to hear. "Sometimes I mumble when I'm not lecturing," he says, feeling like a kid being smart to his mother. "Maybe it's my ear, this ear," she says, but she doesn't mean it. Bert smiles kindly. He hears almost nothing. Stanley thinks Bert is eighty-six but Flo corrects him, the Colonel is only going on eighty-six. He raises the Chinese flag of colored fishes from his dock at Calm Harbor when his sons come to visit and now Stanley is one of them. He shows Stanley a photograph of his college wrestling team in which, very lithe, he looks much like he does now in his eighties, and tells Stanley what became of each of the fellows on the team in later life.

The coach was a Polish chap, who gave them a little wine before each match to prime the blood. Flo broils them a sea trout caught by Bert's friend Al, also in his eighties, who still fishes the Gulf alone in his boat. "I'm glad you don't still do that," Flo says to Bert. He hears. "Why?" he says, smiling in tender anticipation. "I would worry about you so much," she says.

Outside on the porch of the stilted house the night is dark and fresh with wind, and Stanley can see white flashes of birds smaller than gulls diving for fish and wonders how they see them. From the house and boat and marina lights across the cut he can see the channel waves accordioning in the wind. Way off, he sees the lights of a ship in the intercoastal waterway. Stanley thinks of Spain and of England, of all the waters he has been on in life and in his reading and imagining. "Aren't you coming in?" his mother calls.

Stanley goes in to kiss her, as she lies in her bed in this house set by the water that she has so unexpectedly come to. Her brace is off. She looks young again and like she did when she was his mother and he was a boy. "Good fish," he says.

"I forgot you don't eat butter," she says.

"Sometimes I do," he says.

But soon Mack says to Stanley, "I think we need to get them out of there. They're barely making it. It's dangerous."

The Colonel had built railings in the house so Flo could cling to them and get around. Bert drives too fast to the grocery store and pushes his cart at a run and piles cheap frozen dinners and canned stuff and six-packs of Carling in it. In the evening they watch the news on television and discuss it. In the morning he walks around the perimeter of Calm Harbor, around the weathered houses built on slips with small boats tied to the docks. He visits with the few people who are out and with the gulls who always have opinions and returns and tells her the bits of news and his observations and then retells the old family stories about the Williamses and the Grants in Galena and so on. Flo listens and smiles. Stanley has wanted them to stay at Calm Harbor for as long as at all possible, but when he visits again Flo can no longer make it up and down the outside stairs and is housebound, and as he goes to the store with the Colonel he is frightened by his driving.

So Mack and Stanley drive them in a van up to a retirement village near the medical center in Dallas.

Stanley's mother goes at once into the nursing unit, permanently on oxygen. Calm Harbor has worn her out. Emphysema narrows her world down to a tunnel with constricting walls.

The Colonel takes a small apartment in the complex. He roams the corridors and grounds. Many evenings Stanley goes to see his mother and then goes to have a drink of J. W. Dant with the Colonel before dinner and to listen to the stories. After dinner the Colonel goes to sit with Flo.

When Stanley gets the call from the nursing unit it is about nine o'clock at night. He drives to the Oakwood Village East. He goes into his mother's room.

What was Flo is sitting up with pillows behind her in her hospital bed dressed in a pink gown and her faded kimono, her hair awry as if brushed by an antic stylist. Her eyes are open but blank, the depth of blue gone from them. Her mouth is partly open as if she would like to say something. Looking at her objectively and not as her son, Stanley sees her, this scene, as ghastly. She seems to be stiffening as he looks at her. He wonders if the Colonel, sitting in a chair just beside and close to her in the raised bed, knows that she is dead.

The Colonel smiles at him, unclasps his hands and turns to look at her. "Why," he says, "isn't she lovely? She has never looked more beautiful."

Stanley wants to scream.

CHAPTER

4

ALWAYS SUSCEPTIBLE TO VISIONS anyway, now Stanley drifts and dreams, going to his sacred place, to connect again with it and with himself, and with those who dwell and roam there.

Strangely, Stanley first sees Polo's hand.

Polo has a withered hand.

Stanley thinks it is a war wound, but Polo has never said so.

He rubs the withered, finger-lacking hand with his good hand that is plenty capable of work and for directing others and that raises the bourbon and the wine in the evening.

"Hey, Stanley," Polo always greets him, "how's the old hen?"

Stanley doesn't tell Olive that this is how Polo refers to her. He refers to all not young married women, except his own *esposa,* in that way. He never refers to his *esposa* at all, just defers to her, obeys her, of course within the established limits of being a man, *un hidalgo, jefe* of the work force of the fort, caretaker, boss, *el viejo con los cojones.*

36

Polo gets Stanley's name right, anyway. Or does he? Maybe he thinks "Stanley" is his last name. Once Stanley overheard Polo say to the fort director, "Hey, Roberts, that damn Stanley don't know how to do nothing, eh?"

A little later Polo says to Stanley, "Hey, Stanley, that damn Roberts, you know, he's a ding-a-ling, man. He takes hold of that wire when we're having the power outrage and she comes back up, the power, and he stands there with it and don't let go, I thought he's going to be electrocute, burn right up, I never laugh so much, what a ding-a-ling. Eh?"

Polo's family helped kill Governor Bent when he tried to take over the territory for the U.S. and his bunch fought poor young Captain Godwin when he marched on them and the Indians in the pueblo. Killed him, too. So of course they named the fort for him, for Captain Godwin. Polo's family has been here two hundred years. Polo does not like to report to *anglos*.

Maybe he thinks the fort should have been named for his family, for the old relative that had Bent's head.

Through all the years, anyway, there's no doubt who runs the fort.

The years! So many years gone by, Stanley muses.

It is my psychic home, that place, so beautiful there, with two streams flowing through it, in the forest, the snow-covered mountains, rising off north of the lovely valley—I keep it with me. It—

Yes, Stanley. Yes, indeed, says Stanley to himself. Tra la la. Dum da dum dum. Doodle-dee-dee. . . . *It's twi-light time . . .*

When Stanley is a young man and first comes to this rebuilt old fort from which the dragoons used to march out in sparkling snow or thundering rain or sun on quaking aspens to chase the Apaches and usually to be killed by them, so many years ago, Polo is here already with his *esposa*, the slender Esmeralda, the chimney builder.

"Hey, Stanley," says Polo then, that first time, "they want us, me and you, man, to serve the drinks. Eh?"

Serving the visiting brass at the fort, which in summer months is a research and teaching place for his university, Stanley stands behind a long plank table, open sky above, ladling out margaritas they have thrown together in a washtub into cups for Professor This and Chairman That and Dean Whooo and Provost Prigg and the lovely Mrs. Longnose Sharptongue, wifey to the dean.

"Hey, Stanley," Polo says. "You ever hear this story? I hear it in the army, you know, man. This guy, see, this colored guy, I don't know what color, maybe he's a black guy or a Chinaman or a Spanish guy like me, *como*, they make him be the cook of the camp, because he is the colored guy, see? Eh? So pretty soon, after a little while, maybe a couple weeks, he's been cooking and they say, 'Hey, man, you're doing a good job as cook, maybe we'll treat you better, treat you just like all the other guys, you keep on doing a good job, eh?' So this guy says, 'OK, thank you very much, *chingan*, you treat me like a regular guy, maybe I quit pissing in the soup.' Eh?"

"Is that what this makes you feel like?" Stanley says.

Polo rubs his withered hand and scoops up some liquid in a cup with his good hand and sloshes it around in his mouth and spits it out, just missing the rim of the metal tub full of the yellow mixture by their feet.

"Maybe," he says.

Now Stanley says a prayer for Polo and his withered hand and for the frail-looking strong hands of Esmeralda who so flawlessly shapes and constructs the corner fireplaces of this country, and thinks of his father, who is astounded when for some perverse reason both his sons became English professors. Stanley apologizes to his father, who struggled to survive in the Great Depression of the '30s and who always tells his sons Stanley and Barry, whatever else they do in life, they must learn a trade, must know how to do something real that they can make a living doing in the next depression, always on its way. Barry is to learn to be an electrician, Stanley, less smart in his father's opinion, less able to master electricity or plumbing, is to be a bricklayer. Barry is not a bad electrician by now, but Stanley—how predictable, alas—has never learned or even tried to learn to lay a brick. With his one capable hand Polo can do real things, things Stanley cannot fathom with springs and pumps and tractors and backhoes and wells and roofs and vega ceilings and toilets . . .

Off the highway, and nestled in the soft green hills at the edge of the national forest, this compound is isolated from the town, from tourists and all but the most curious passersby. Its buildings have been hand-raised by Roberts, the archaeologist director, from the old army drawings. It is simple, a square figure eight, of roughout logs and chinking, with some rough cabins down farther, by the *río*. Stanley looks at the little twisted trees and the gray-green chamisa bushes covering the land. Polo says his father said there used to be rich grasses here where it is now all chamisa. Inside the compound, now, Roberts tries to keep soft grass growing in the open areas ringed by the labs and classrooms.

The smell is of real, clear air, and spicy, of altitude and cedar.

There is much silence, looking up to hills and to the mountains way beyond, the silence centered in them. Every day the pattern of sun and rain, of clouds, of warm and cool, is different but the same. The colors can all disappear, or be incredible—so black and pink and gold at sunset that you begin to understand bad art, and why the artists do not understand that it is bad . . .

Over across the highway and up a dirt road and over a plank bridge where the *río* crosses again are the ruins of an ancient pueblo, on the highest plateau of this land. There—Stanley sees it in his mind's eye now—is the compact area of round excavations that had been houses, their rooms exposed, and storage pits. In the center at the highest point is the hole entrance going down into the central kiva. One time Stanley let himself down the ladder into the small underground room and felt half man, half animal, felt sacredness, felt himself eternal yet terribly mortal standing on the packed dirt floor in the airless musty coolness with close dark walls around where the yellow, red and blue designs had been painted.

Now he does not go in that direction but turns and heads up towards the ridge, leaving the *río,* going through a little meadow and into the trees, going higher.

He is going down a path, surrounded by little feathery bushes, small trees, whispering cedar and giant gnarled trees, ponderosas, some crashed and fallen to the needled ground, to the river beyond the rust-red rushes.

It is the old nature trail by the fort. He has walked along it, walked upon it all the years. Years ago they had put up signs along the path identifying the flora. Then the flora shifted, changed, sometimes disappeared. Yet some remains. He pauses, listening to the water sound, looking at a bent gray weathered board. The weathered sign says: *Artemista Tridentata*—"Big Sagebrush." It remains, the bush is by the sign.

He hears the sounds of the cedars whispering, telling something they know to each other and to him. He has felt, always along this trail, that they are alive. Now he knows they are and that the cedars know some secret they are trying to tell him . . .

He turns and sees old Bob—Jesus, old Bob Kettle—sitting on a stump along the path, smoking his pipe and combing through the snarls in his white beard with his fingers just as he always did. They have been together in the Mexican desert, Bob the anthropologist, Stanley studying folklore, filling dark nights as still as the desert with talk.

"Don't you recall, damn it, Stanley?" old Bob says. "Now I'm sure you do, you were putting it out of your so-called mind, weren't you, old bean? Hell, I lived with it, Stanley, you remember, lived with it, metastasized, nine years. Wouldn't let the bastards cut on me." Nods to him and puffs his pipe.

Stanley is embarrassed, not knowing if old Bob is still alive, living with it, but doesn't ask. It's a chilly, half raw morning, Stanley thinks it's morning from the level of the sun and is glad and happy that it's not raining along the trail. Now the water is rushing below him down off the trail in the *río*.

But *bingo* it all turns stark and chillier still, the colors fade back, the greens and blues go mute, the dapple of sun grays, it all turns stark and like an etching in gray and black and white. The next weathered board along the path says: *Chrysothamnus Nauseosis*.

Also remaining: small gray patch of rabbitbrush.

Now Mack, his friend and brother Mack, comes running down the trail in his jogging shorts and T-shirt and running shoes. He looks as lean as when he was Cassius in their school play, "yon Cassius," his face is like a scythe, he nods at Stanley running by but doesn't smile.

"I'm looking for my buddy," Mack says to Stanley, "looking for my buddy."

Legs and arms pumping, he goes by, doesn't smile or wink, goes on down the trail, legs pumping, pumping, pumping.

Stanley looks at the dead gray rushes by the river, his heart cold, his pulse stopped; but in a moment they turn back on, the rushes gain color, they become burnt orange, their red tips flame, the cedars framing them turn green again, as on the path a guy comes running after Mack, running lightly, a Jewish-looking guy with a beard and a lean body, running in a loincloth and his sandals.

This guy smiles at Stanley. His smile is radiant. Also it is kind. His eyes glow and he looks pure, his form is pure, running by. Stanley hopes he will catch Mack. Running by he speaks to Stanley, looking at him sideways as he passes.

"What do you say?" he says. "What do you say?" he says to Stanley.

Later, an instant or a long time later, Stanley thinks he sees young Captain Godwin sitting by the *río* down from the trail, sitting on the ground by the rushing little river in his uniform with brass buttons shined. He also wears a beard, light chestnut, and is a handsome fellow. They have named the fort for him in 1846 after he is killed by the Hispanics and the Indians and they say he walks the trail and the woods and along the water's edge and walks the high ridge at night, overseeing the fort.

Stanley would like to talk to Captain Godwin but is very tired and thinks he will not do it now. Instead he looks around, stopping, sitting now alongside the trail. Many of the trees here are shattered, the smaller scraggly ones standing in among them. He sees a huge gray trunk, fungus- and vine-covered in the tangle of forest. It is like a great shattered penis set on a withered scrotum, impotent, its chestnut gone . . .

Stanley sits listening to the river flowing. The rushes beside the river are blood-colored. He can hear the flow, it goes down and then goes up as it goes by. Godwin's gone. Stanley looks to a green treed ridge beyond the trail, and on to the snowcapped sacred mountain, the sun-streaked chill and lovely morning, the mountain topped with snow, the leopard surely there . . .

Ah, just to doze, now, perhaps forever. ("'Forever,' what a word," he hears his brother Barry say. "I never use it.") But he hears Olive's soft beautiful voice. Bless her, she always chides him for his naps, his sacred little dozes in the daytime. She is saying he must wake up. But it's pleasant, just to nap the tag end of life away . . . and pleasant here under sun both cool and warm, the mountain sun, God's wind in your ear, the up and down, the flowing of the *río* . . .

He hopes that Mack's buddy will catch him, that Mack will not have to run—you know—that word that Barry will not use . . . *forever* . . .

The cedars whisper. What are they saying?
Stan-ley. Stan-ley—
"Morris? Mor-ris? That your name?"

CHAPTER

5

STANLEY STRUGGLES TO AWAKEN really, from the surgery and from his dreams.

He wakes to a blur of light. There is a bank of white lights in the room. He closes his eyes, then opens them to the blur. The light is shining from above. There is no one here with him. He thinks he is alive but all alone, or maybe he is in limbo. He is in a cocoon of soft diffused white light. He closes his eyes and sees light behind his lids.

For a while, in the mountains there, he has been blinded, has taught blind. When Olive comes she tells him he is foolish to try to stay and teach not being able to read, to see. She is so very right.

Where is she? Where is Olive?

Where is he?

When he wakes again he is still not sure of the form of things. There is still too much light, but he makes out shapes. He is not in limbo but in a room. There is a tall creature of some sort like a praying mantis in a corner. It has several arms or tentacles and a bowing head and appears to be something dark and feathery. It waves an arm at him.

Suddenly a large dark form looms over him.

"I be Harriett," she says, and softly takes his hand. Now he feels he is full of tubes, bound to a bed, his legs sheathed and bound. She places the fingers of his left hand around a ball, a rubber bulb. He presses it.

"You be having any pain you just press that," she says.

He feels no pain. He feels nothing whatsoever. He presses the bulb, pumps and pumps and pumps it. It is glorious to have it in your hand and to be pressing it.

He hears her laugh. "It regulates," she says.

Later he opens his eyes and a boy comes into focus. He's a red-headed kid with a cap on backwards like Leo Gorcey of the Dead End Kids.

"I brought you my late paper," he says. "How you doing?"

"Just put it— Just leave it— Thank you—" Stanley says.

The boy smiles. "I just like thought I'd come by. I'm surprised some of the others aren't here. Sorry the paper's late. I need a B in this course to graduate so I hope you don't count off for it being late."

Stanley doesn't know if this kid is real. Is he a real present student of his or is he somehow all the students he's ever had in all the years of teaching taking this symbolic, dreamlike form?

"Well, we'll see," says Stanley. "We'll see about it—"

"Jim," the kid says, and smiles, and tosses the red hair out of his eyes.

The next time he wakes Olive is there with his friend Andy, the chaplain of his university.

"Well, well," Andy says, "are you feeling as well as you look?"

"Feeling no pain," says Stanley, pumping the morphine bulb.

"We may have an addict on our hands before we get him out of here," says the chaplain, chuckling.

"They had you in intensive care, just for observation," Olive says when the chaplain leaves. "We were waiting. You came through fine. Andy said a prayer. He was so concerned. I tried to reassure him."

Stanley laughs. He feels it.

"I don't think you're supposed to laugh," Olive says. "How do you like your orchid? It's from the Zimmermans. Isn't it gorgeous? I don't know a thing about taking care of orchids."

Stanley sees that the thing in the corner is a tall orchid plant. Its drooping head is the orchid.

In the afternoon all comes clearer and in the evening, with the morphine every fifteen minutes, he is clear but floating. He feels fine and quite poetic, he and dear old Coleridge. Xanadu and pleasure dome and all that . . .

He convinces Olive he is fine, that he will not need her for the night. He does not want her to have to sleep in the chair or on a cot. He's fine. She's had an anxious, tiring time waiting.

He has a hideous night.

It's dark. He doesn't know where anything is. He has tubes in him and flounders in the bed and cannot get comfortable, and the tubes tangle. Suddenly he is aware of the catheter in his penis. Spasms, surges come in his penis. He is terrified. He calls out. He can't find the button to call for help. He must get up, get out of bed—

A man comes in and thrusts him roughly back.

He lies in the night in the dark, disoriented, dreading the spasms, not knowing his context, the boundaries, uncomfortable.

In early morning the surges in his penis come more regularly and with horrible urgency. Suddenly he feels himself wetting, wetting everything— He looks and sees the fluid mixed with blood— Dear Jesus, is the catheter out? Is he dying? Is he going to bleed to death from his poor damn penis—?

Bellowing, he presses the call button.

After the nurses get him hooked up properly again, the dark man who was so rough with him in the night comes in. His name badge says *Joseph*. He is haughty, looks Indian Indian.

"I am familiar with the circumstances of procedures such as yours." He seems to sneer at Stanley, as if beholding a weakling. "You must not panic. Often there is a brief period of spasm in such cases."

"Procedures such as yours"? *Procedures?* Seems like a full-fledged operation to Stanley. What does this superior fellow know about it anyway? Where does he get off being so condescending to a patient? Is he a Sikh? Is this Inder Singh's long-lost brother? Same arrogance, same sneer . . .

"The nurses at the station are concerned that you are spasming so much," Olive says when she arrives. "I'll stay with you tonight."

More flowers arrive. Sprays and pots and baskets of flowers. They all look alike to Stanley. Olive says they must remember who sent what. Stanley says he will leave that up to her. She says he's sounding a little more like himself.

Visitors come through the day.

It's funny who comes to visit you, who doesn't. It's surprising. Of course all the close friends and the nearby family come. Most of the close friends, mostly couples, come and stand in a circle around the pot plants and flowers they bring and don't stay long out of consideration, seeing Stanley writhe and gasp every so often. Stanley's sister Little Dear, his younger sister who also lives outside Dallas, is one of the first to appear in the morning. She tells him news of their brother Barry, who has called her from his home in New Jersey to ask about Stanley. She says that Barry considers a prostate removal to be a ridiculous operation, he would never do it. (Barry does not tell her what he would do, but she and Stanley understand what Barry means: he does not countenance cancer in the first place, therefore for him it does not exist and is no problem. Barry took the same attitude to their mother's emphysema in the period before she died. His foot, Stanley speculates, Barry's now lost foot, must be another matter. He must pursue this with his brother in the future, philosophically.) Little Dear reports that Barry is seasoning his stump. He is seasoning it in preparation for the arrival and fitting, in a few months, of a prosthetic foot. This will arrive at a cost of some five thousand dollars. Barry has mentioned this figure to her in awe. For this reason he is postponing his next scheduled train trip. Their brother Barry spends his free summers and his boodle whenever he can in rail travel.

"That is a dear foot," Stanley says.

"Our father would say, 'That foot is costing him an arm and a leg,'" says Little Dear. Stanley laughs, then feeling he is going to rip open, stops. Under the bandage there is reputed to be a scar that best not be ripped open by random levity. Under the padded area he knows he is slit from belly button to groin, zipped back, everything, we trust, rearranged correctly.

"The boy's name is Jim Riddle," Olive reports, looking at the paper the student has left. Stanley has a confused sense of just who the students are in his class presently as opposed to last summer and terms and eras past. But he knows that Joe Green is teaching them in his absence, that they are in good hands. "It's a paper, let's see," she says, "on Hemingway. On the polarity—that wouldn't be the right word, would it?—of Jake's condition of impotence and the narrative viewpoint in *The Sun Also Rises*."

"How appropriate."

"Don't you dare let yourself think like that!" Her eyes blaze at him.

The president of Stanley's university, Highland U., comes to visit. This is an honor. Stanley sits up as straight as he can. O. Arthur Biggs is a distinguished man with one sound eye and one nonfunctioning eye, a physical feature they have in common. Also they are the same age. The favorite author of O. Arthur Biggs is Rudyard Kipling. He brings Stanley a volume of Kipling's more inspirational poetry, properly inscribed. He sets his merry sea-green eye on him. Two months ago he had a heart attack and Stanley had tried to go see him in the hospital here but he was in intensive care and they would not let him in. But Art knows he tried.

"How's the search for the new dean?" Stanley says, gritting his teeth, a surge coming on.

"About the same as when you came in here," O. Arthur says, never one to suffer dullards. "Nationwide search, nitwits, incompetents and loons springing to the fore. I told you about the guy who applied who said God led him to us."

"How was the hotshot from—where?—who wanted everything to be interactive so we could embrace the twenty-first century by being a virtual university on the worldwide web?"

"Don't mention it. It gives me indigestion. That's my heart attack of the future. He didn't have as much sense as that bunch of daylilies there. Considerably less. Had no sense of doing budget." Art is keen on budgets. "Did hear from our old pal Jack Bompers though."

Jack Bompers is the former dean, gone off to Virginia, just had his prostate removed.

"How's Jack doing?" Stanley says, with trepidation.

"OK. OK, I guess. Sounds pretty good. Wants to tell you all about it. You want to know his PSA count? I didn't. He's telling me about his goddamn penile exercises, over the phone, a big donor is waiting to come in the office, I thought I should talk to Jack for old times' sake. Listen, Morris, if and when you get out of here, will you please have the grace and decency for God's sake to keep your penile progress or lack of it to yourself?"

Stanley promises he will. And he will, if all goes well. He wonders what is bothering Jack Bompers.

O. Arthur Biggs, he thinks, knows that Morris is his last and not his first name. President Biggs, being the one guy totally responsible, with ten million things on his mind, has the habit of calling everybody by surname. He is a lawyer, has been in and out of government, business, and academe; he makes connections and gets a handle on people by their last names, Stanley thinks, like a lawyer, like Biggs, Bompers, Godwin, Riddle, Morris, and Kipling.

Biggs seems frail as he nods at Stanley and departs. He is still recovering from his heart attack and looks, oh, tentative, just a bit unsure as he turns and walks away. Oh my. President Biggs is tired, of course, for he has plunged right back in. It's a new academic year and he has just been through all the pro forma opening rituals of the university and must now turn to putting "asks" on prospective major donors and firing the football coach, unless a miracle occurs and

50

they win more than one game this season, and hiring a new basketball coach, probably a short one this time since the short ones seem
to win more games than the tall ones, and facing off the key alumni
who do not in their hearts embrace "diversity" in the student body
and the key trustees who wish to undertake "reengineering" of the
university, and placating the faculty, whose raise will be 2–3 percent
again, and the students, who are certain he wants to do away with
the "Greek" system of elitist white sororities and fraternities, which
O. Arthur Biggs would do in a flash if he thought he could get away
with it: all the relentless duties of a contemporary university president, for which he will need immensely more energy than he seems
to possess at the moment.

And Stanley: he should be there too, in the arena of the classroom, and the Faculty Senate, and his half-dozen committees, and
working on his new book, back in the damn saddle, on the campus
doing—his life!

Whoa, Stanley!

Yesterday you were euphoric, so happy just to be alive.

Today you're jumping the gun—with the gun in spasms—

Face it, pal. Here you are.

And Art Biggs is nursing a weakened heart. And brother Barry
is up in Jersey "seasoning" his stump. And Mack—is gone.

A certain phase of deterioration of males of a certain age seems
to have set in.

He reaches for the Kipling. He needs for something, if even just an
image, to come "up like thunder" across some bay . . .

He is in a reverie about O. Arthur and the appeal of Kipling to him when an unexpected figure pops into the room. It is old Clancy, good Lord, Stanley has not seen him for years, maybe a dozen years, he hardly recognizes him. Clancy has gone bald, has large hairs sprouting from his ears. Old "Lewis and Clark" Clancy, the former professor of geography in their university. He has white spittle on his mouth and his eyes seem unfocused. He wears a heavy cardigan sweater with holes in its sleeves. He must be very old by now as he points his finger in at Stanley.

"Young Morris!" he accuses.

"Yes. Yes? How are you, Howard? I'm pleased, and surprised, that—"

"Just in the building. Nothing to do with you," says old Professor Clancy, whose academic discipline does not even exist in their curriculum anymore, "geography" now for years absorbed by the discipline of geological sciences, if it even remains in that.

"Cancer? Cancer?"

Stanley just stares back at him, the rude old fool.

"Did they get it all?"

"Did they get it all?" My God! What a question! What sane person would ask it of you? The one question so terribly inappropriate, so terribly appropriate.

"It is in question," Stanley replies. "We are awaiting the pathology report."

"Ah— Yes? Well, then, good luck. It's in no doubt about my wife. She's dying of it down the hall. See you, young Morris— Or— Is your name Stanley? You helped ruin the curriculum, I know that, you helped do in the sciences, with that 'general education' crap—"

The old man is weeping as he turns and leaves. Crying for his dying wife.

Stanley vows that in this new life of his he will be kinder, try not to jump to judgment, though it will be difficult.

"Did they get it all?"

My God, thinks Stanley, did they?

The third day is a Saturday. Stanley is still having spasms, occasional surges in the penis, and the doctor is coming by. But on the positive side, they take the IV out. He can have something to eat, or at least to drink. They put him on a liquid diet.

They are waiting for the pathology report.

Have they sent it to Mars?

There even is the prospect in the near future of a bowel movement.

In preparation for this great event Stanley gets up, puts his new striped robe on over the little backless gown, and moves around a little. Harriett comes to have him sit and bathe. The ever-present drainage bag, colorful with liquid, sits full at his feet. It is now the color of California rosé wine. She disconnects and empties it, flushing, then reconnects. She smiles her big-tooth smile at him, pointing to the bag, his appendage for the foreseeable future.

"That be Priscilla," she says.

"Oh," says Stanley, "I don't think I'll call it that."

Harriett laughs. "Well, it be Priscilla," she says, plugging in his razor so he can shave. He doesn't tell her his favorite aunt is named Priscilla.

For lunch he is brought a hard roll, mashed potatoes, a breaded chop, and jello.

"I am supposed to be on a liquid diet," he explains. "See, it says so, right here. I can't have this."

The attendant shakes her head and takes the tray away, does not return.

Diamond, the R.N. from the nurses' station, comes in to take his temperature, pulse, and blood pressure readings. "It's all fine. You're doing great," she says. She is a beautiful black Diamond. He starts to tell her about the food, but what the hell, he isn't hungry.

Later a nice P.C.A., Veronica, helps him walk a little up and down the hall. They laugh together going up and down as his bowels begin to unkink and come alert.

Hoo—oot— Hoo—hoot—hooo! Stanley's bowels rumbling; Stanley and his companion laughing, they make their way like a tug-boat by the doors of startled patients.

In the evening Joseph brings him a tray, removes the cover with a flourish. On the plate are beef tips and string beans, looking tough as leather, and what looks to be the same damn roll, hard as a rock.

"Look here," says Stanley. "Liquid, get it? Liquid, liquid, liquid."

"Oh, why do you make such a fuss?" Joseph says, sneering at him, as if he were the veritable Oliver Twist. "This is the general diet."

"I am supposed to be on a liquid diet."

"Oh, why do you worry? (Extra work for all.)" He says this as an aside as if he is speaking to some rational third person who might happen to be in the room with them. Insufferable!

"Listen, you—Joseph—"

"Quiet. Do not worry. Oh, if you do not know, I will tell you. Yes? It is the same, it is the same. Soft is the same as general. You will see. You will see."

54

After a while they come and take the tray away. Imperious Sikh. Stanley must deal with him. Hears him now, declaiming, strutting up and down the hall from now to midnight as if he owns it, which of course he does. Must find a way to deal with him. Stanley wishes to be kinder in this new life, but he is not Jesus. Hell, Jesus would be angrier than Stanley—

He calls Olive, tells her to bring a large Coke and maybe a pint of vodka when she comes. She laughs, as if she thinks he's joking.

The poor woman down the hall starts shouting epithets and shrieking. All day she moans and cries and mumbles obscenities in the evening and during the night from time to time she turns to shrieks and louder epithets and screams.

"What is her problem?" he asked Harriett the day before.

"She be confused," Harriett explained.

Dr. Lester Miller comes swinging in. He is on his way to hunting doves or something but wants to take a look at his pal Stanley. Martz or Wu will be along tomorrow. Miller's dark eyes and small strong hands take a look at Stanley, seeing what's what. Looks good. Nice piece of work.

"Sorry about the spasms," he says. "That's not unusual. The spasm is in your bladder, you know, not in the penis, as it seems to you. Physiological reality is seldom what it seems, eh? I'm giving you some pills, these big babies. That usually works. Want you to really try, though, to hold the spasms back. You want to get control as much as you can now. Too much surging and it might spoil the nice repair work we did putting it all back together, don't you see."

Stanley looks at him a little bleakly, this kind man who terrified him so at first.

"This is a time of healing, now, Professor," Lester Miller says.

"You must relax now and envision control—gain control and think of healing. We cut some nerves, you know. It must all come back together. You let yourself heal and be whole."

Stanley nods. Dr. Lester Miller is a savior, a genius at his craft, a caring, skilled physician.

But this is not exactly, for Stanley, a time of healing. It is a time of tension, tyranny and stress.

That night he rings and Joseph comes and helps him to the toilet. There is a glorious flood of bowel matter, to a Valkyrie chorus.

"I have several Indian friends," says Stanley, back in bed as Joseph turns to go.

"Oh? Yes?"

"Yes. My particular friend is the distinguished anglophone novelist and political activist Nayantara Sahgal. And her husband Nirmal Mangat-Rai, said to be the Jefferson of his country."

"Yes? Yes. I know of her. Yes. I have read her novel in which the subject is *suttee*, as she is contrasting the old and the new India. Mangat-Rai is a great man, of my region. I am from Punjab. You know these two well?"

"Yes. They have visited in my university. How long have you been in this country, here?"

"Oh, twenty years. Nearly twenty years by now."

"Do you like it here? Is it home by now?"

"Oh. 'Home' has little concept for me. I like being on this floor, in charge, where I have respect."

"I understand. I feel the same about my place in the university. In fact, it's so secure one tends to feel insecure outside its pleasant confines."

"Yes," Joseph says.

In a while he returns bearing a tray.

"I have brought you some ice water and some orange juice in case you desire liquids after I am gone off shift. Just call me, meanwhile, if you need me," Joseph says.

"Thank you," Stanley says.

That night after midnight, with no one's permission, he takes Priscilla and walks down the hall all the way to the ice machine and gets some ice. At the ice station he sees in the shadows another figure, perhaps also a patient. This fellow looks like the same fellow in his vision of Mack and his buddy running by but is now clad all in white. Gently glowing, he smiles at Stanley and raises a knotty hand to him, thumb up, as if in encouragement. Stanley nods to him and with the ice returns slowly along the hall singing and dancing to "Me and My Shadow" in his mind.

It is a great adventure.

CHAPTER

6

SUNDAY MORNING, ANXIOUS, STILL a bit foggy, Stanley sits up in the chair in the room and tries to read the newspaper. He finds the Metro section dreary, the national pages confusing, the international news tragic if not terrifying, the business section arcane, the sports pages infuriating. Can't anyone simply cover a game anymore, tell what happened play by play? He does not care about the bums' contracts or the players' negotiations with the owners. In all, Stanley finds it as old Henry David said so long ago in *Walden,* "sedulous gingerbread, baked daily."

About church time a little man pops in. His mission is serious and he is earnest, but he seems somehow comic to Stanley.

"I am so-and-so," he says, garbling his own name. The hospital has sent him, or as he seems to say, something like, "indubitably in the employ of this swell facility so dedicated to Hippocratic health that you are now enjoying."

Stanley laughs, rather startling the fellow. Stanley decides to name him Tupman, the fellow should be in Dickens. Stanley dresses him in piebald, striped pants and checked coat, and puts a stage hat in one hand. Yes, Tupman, Hubert Tupman.

"Is all well with you here in these commodious accommodations?" Tupman says. The sun is streaming in the window and the fellow looks dramatically to the excellent view of the busy parking lot below and at the state of the hospital art furniture and furnishings, and to the technical apparatus and beyond to the sparkling bathroom. "How's your room? You know, it's a nice big single for your money!"

Oh yes, Stanley nods. Large enough for twelve visitors at once if you stack them around the walls and seat some in the window bay.

With a flourish of hand Tupman produces a sheet of computer flimsy. He moves a step closer to Stanley, dramatically careful not to fall off his stage into the orchestra pit, and peruses the page as if 'twere the Magna Carta.

"Your part," he says, "of this fair and comprehensive invoice or bill, whatever you want to call it, which of course does not reflect the remarkable and we are sure impeccable artistry of your surgeons or the empathic expertise of the anesthesiologist, the guy what 'overed over your every unconscious breath, Mr. Stanley, is nineteen thousand dollars." He beams. "So how would you like to pay?"

"If you will just reach in the drawer there and hand me my wallet, Hubert old boy, I'll pay you in cash."

"Ha! Ha, ha. You joke, of course. A little spoofery, eh? We know of course no one can afford to be in a hospital without copious insurance and you are PPO Uni-Pro Coalition, Mr.—Professor—is it Doctor Stanley?"

To hell with it, Stanley thinks, name-wise. Maybe they'll charge it to this Morris Stanley.

"Yes. Not medical. Philosophy."

"Ah! Well, what a pleasure, sir, to adumbrate you, here in your fine room on this fine fall day, of the nature of these so-far charges that you are racking up with us!" Or some such. "Philosophy. Of course! There are more—things—in your philosophy, Malvolio— than we—can comprehend in this too too sad fleshliness of our stay on heaven and earth—"

"You got that right," Stanley thinks. Or nearly. Good try, anyway. As the overarticulating fellow smiles and turns, rubs his hand now like Heep, and dances out the door.

He hardly knows how to tell Olive about the fellow when she arrives, so he doesn't. When Harriett comes in she says the Confused Woman has gone home.

"Did she recover?"

"No. She still crazy."

Later a rather large Asian chap with *Doctor Wu* lettered on his starched white jacket comes briskly in. "I am Wu," he says. "Assisted with you in operation, little bit. Pretty slick. Dr. Miller got great hands. Right? You doing good, eh? I think so. Pathology looks OK. Looks like it didn't spread, got it. So we can put up some balloons, eh?"

Stanley gives a great shudder of relief. Tears well in his eyes, as he looks at Olive in her chair by the window. Dr. Wu thumps on his stomach. "But I got to give you a CAT scan, I'm afraid. Young doctor, checkup fella, plays shortstop for us so no balls get through the infield, he thinks he felt something, you know? You are pretty thick right along in here."

"Couldn't it be that I'm just pretty thick?"

"Maybe. I don't know. Young doctor says maybe aneurism. CAT scan."

"Oh, for pity's sake," says Olive. "I told you to lose that middle, Stanley."

"Is that serious?"

"You kidding? If it bursts it'll kill you dead. Don't you remember, Uncle Judd had that operation for a stomach aneurism? They got it just in time."

"I had forgotten that," says Stanley.

An orderly comes and lifts Stanley, his moment of relief so quickly gone, onto a trolley or gurney or whatever it is and wheels him quickly through the halls, down an elevator and into the bowels of the building. He is delivered to a large machine operated by a tall woman of stern, relentless visage. He is tossed from the trolley under the machine so roughly that he fears his incision has popped open. He feels a searing pain in his stomach, then a terrible pulling pain as the fellow starts to wheel the trolley away with his drainage bag still on it, the tube and bag stuck under the side bar—"*Owww— Weeee*—" He imagines his penis will be pulled off, will pop off— He screams and screams again—

"Sorry," says the attendant.

"I just had an operation. Jesus . . ."

"Sorry. I didn't know," the young man says. He's a boy with pimples. He looks really sorry.

The tall lean woman comes over and prods and pokes him on his back into the position she wants him in.

"Be still," she says. "I'll tell you when to breathe and change positions. If you don't do exactly what I say right when I tell you we'll have to do it all over."

"You almost killed me," Stanley says.

"Not likely," she says, smiling for the first time, if a bit sadistically, and taps him lightly on the arm like the endearing gesture of a lover who must leave your side. "I'm glad the catheter held. That would have been a mess."

She goes to caress her dials, starts the machine and her commands. He lies and listens and breathes and twists as told, his penis sore and aching worse than from any lover's passion spent.

It's not as bad as the time before. His head is not under the damnable machine. When his face itches he can scratch it. He gets through it. Jesus, Jesus, Wu said the pathology is OK. This—the other thing—must be a joke.

The procedure ends. His stern angular lover turns from him to other duties without a word. The boy wheels him back to his room very carefully.

Sunday evening he is calmer. A large, handsome young doctor comes and sits at the foot of his bed and tells him with a wry smile that he has no stomach aneurism. Stanley thanks him for this information as he departs.

"I told them you were just thick in the middle," Olive says. "When we get you home, and all recovered, we should try to do something about that, shouldn't we?"

Stanley makes a face at her. As far as he personally is concerned, "we" do not wish to make any big commitments right now for the future. His body has done well, he thinks. Every once in a while his leg jerks, a foot pops up and back, or his upper leg tremors. "I am either beginning to relax or having a stroke," he says to Olive.

"Do you want to call the doctor?"

"No!" he says.

Actually he feels younger, physically, than he has for years. His head doesn't ache. His neck isn't stiff. His back isn't strained. His feet don't hurt from bearing too much weight. His eyes aren't strained. For years he has thought maybe he should go to a monastery for a week or so and meditate, or take up a martial art, or treat himself to a week at Fort Godwin without students, have a little rest cure, really relax. He never thought of having a nice little prostate operation to take the strain off the old bod. Ha. Actually Dr. Miller has said there is a lot of stuff to heal, there are a lot of wires cut, a lot of nerves and flow-stuff getting straight again. But he feels no pain, his urine flows free and ever more clear. Yes, urine flow: collecting automatically and abstractly, untroublingly in "Priscilla."

Right in the moment, Sunday evening, few cars in Mr. Tupman's state-of-the-art parking lot below, a pale sun sinking down behind the blue and green and silver buildings with their flat tops or little Victorian caps, he feels that his amazing body is supple, limber as when he was a youth. He is proud of and grateful to this strange thing that transports him, his awkward, bulky body. All the tense time before the operation, he had gone stiff and told the anesthesiologist he had no breathing problems but had gone short of breath from fear— Born sickly, one-eyed, his life a process of building up to strength, his body had not let him down.

And now he vows to keep it pure and supple, limber.

Yes, he will never smoke or drink again. He is sure of that. What else do you need if you have healed, if you have still that portion of your health appropriate to your age? No, though it has been a chief source of peace and relaxation to him all his adult life, he will never smoke, or drink the dreadful numbing booze, again.

This noble thought makes Stanley yearn to be at home in his study, books around him, slowly smoking a Pedro Allones while he sips a glass of The Famous Grouse.

He nods to the tall orchid in the corner, which seems to incline its head to him.

He looks at the cards he has received, from family, friends, and the faculty, a medley of nice people. Here is one from his colleagues on the Faculty Senate: "We the Executive Committee of the Faculty Senate hereby wish you a prompt recovery to full health and a return to your usual cheerful and inspiring demeanor. The vote was 7 to 4."

Ho ho. One of the good old faculty jokes.

The note from his departmental colleague Morrison J. Harrison begins: "Things are a little crazy around here, not to say insane . . ." He shuffles it back into the pack.

Olive interrupts his perusal of the cards.

"Joe Green called. He'll come by tomorrow. He's playing at Dave's Cool tonight. He wants to know if you want him to bring some papers or stories from your classes. Are you ready for that?"

"God, no. I can't even read the newspaper. My eyes focus on it, but I just can't take it in."

"Would you like to watch a little TV? I can't seem to get the new fall lineup straight."

"Hell, no."

"Well, would you like me to leave," she says, "and get out of your hair?"

"No," he says. "Never."

"All right. That's better." Olive goes back to her crossword puzzle.

Stanley picks up a piece of the Sunday paper and tries to scan it.

Dear Lord, here's another train disaster, down south. Amtrak train going over an eighty-year-old steel and wooden bridge over one of those unpronounceable southern rivers. Bridge collapses, at night. Three engines and four cars go in the river. Seven more cars in a tangled wreck. Forty-four passengers dead or unaccounted for. Men, women, children. Babies. Cause: just an old bridge that collapsed. His sister Little Dear and he have been trying to tell their brother Barry not to ride these damn trains for years. No avail. Train going from L.A. to Miami. Oh my. What's the first thing, first time off he gets, that Barry will do when he gets his new foot? Stanley can just see it as a scene in his mind:

In the early morning of a day in spring a tall gentleman of significant height and girth and wearing a prosthetic foot boards the Amtrak train in Philadelphia and repairs to his compartment for the long rail trip westward to Los Angeles.

"I do not believe in train disasters," he says in a brief interview while boarding. "Like cancer, train disasters are not a category in my mind. Travel by train is, statistically and in every other way of computing, ten thousand times safer than air travel. It is twenty thousand times safer than travel by car."

"I have told you a million times not to exaggerate," Stanley hears his brother Barry telling him, referring to this imagined scene, "especially about me. The truth is good enough."

True. No need to embroider Barry. He has in fact traveled thousands of miles over North America on trains, choosing to spend his summers when not teaching and his vacation in this way. (Barry has no present wife and his daughter is grown with a son of her own, the apple of Barry's eye, whom as soon as possible he wishes to initiate into the joy of train travel so that the lad will not only know reality virtually, on a screen, but really, on a rail.) Barry tells of seeing many strange and interesting sights on these travels. He has seen com-pounds and communes in mountains and in deserts, people living in geodesic huts or plastic tent-homes accessible only by helicopter. He has seen people living where there could not possibly be water, and he has seen strange flags flying, as of separated clans or tribes or nations. He has seen, he says, the mythical camels and herds of white horses and prides of mountain lions and magical blue streams and once-occupied towns left abandoned by roads after the once-shiny track was laid through or over hidden valley or mountain ridge. He has seen fire and he has seen rain . . .

Meanwhile, of course, in his college there in the pretty part of New Jersey Barry has a very quiet, ordered life teaching literature and writing, like his brother Stanley.

A couple years ago, before the inroads of the dreadful dia-betes—this anecdote captures it for Stanley—brother Barry, in the spring, takes the train, the Super Sunset Limited, from Philly on out to L.A. He arrives, whether it is morning or evening, and immedi-ately takes his bag and changes trains at the station, onto the Sunrise Limited, for the trip right back to Philly by a different route. It is spring break, and he has papers to grade and not much time for this particular excursion. He settles in his compartment and takes out his bottle of bourbon and pours a toddy, when a man in a suit comes by. "Mr. Barry?" the man says.

"Dr. Morris, to you, sir," Barry says.

"Yes, yes," says the suited, authoritative man. "I am a Federal drug enforcement officer, and I am visiting you this evening because you have just changed trains after a trip across the continent and appear to be heading back where you came from, immediately."

"Yes, sir, that is correct," says Barry.

"Well, sir, we are interested in you because you seem to have the known characteristics of a drug dealer. Yet, I must say, beholding you, sir, I see that you are just a train nut."

"Yes, sir, that is correct," says Barry. "Would you care for a drink of bourbon?"

"Believe I will," the fellow says.

Many years ago, when they were boys, Stanley older by a year than Barry, their parents let them go by train to visit their grandparents in California. That is when Barry's fascination with the train begins. On the trip Stanley loses him, searches car by car in panic, finally finds him in a bathroom holding the flusher on the toilet down, staring at the crossties clipping by on the track below. At every stop, even in the heat of Needles in the desert, the boy Barry gets off the train and on again, loving just the getting off and on, while Stanley, being Stanley, being very mature at ten and sure that if he gets off the train the train will go suddenly on without him, sits in his seat by the window, never leaving his seat except to go to look for Barry.

Dozing off, Stanley remembers the last time he saw Barry, the summer before this fall, when Barry stopped off to visit him and his sister here in the Metroplex, coming very kindly just to visit them.

Barry stays with Little Dear.

Strangely, he arrives by plane.

There has been a strike and they cancel his train. He will have to wait no one knows how long to come by train. So with great protests and courage he flies in to DFW. Little Dear meets him as he staggers off the jetliner. He is wobbling and talking to himself. Counting those he had in the airport lounge and on the plane, he has had six gin martinis. She puts him in her guest room off the kitchen, and he sleeps through the special chicken cacciatore she's made for dinner, sleeps until the next day.

Stanley doesn't see much of Barry on this visit. It's a short visit and Stanley is teaching two evening courses and has some emergency faculty meetings called. Anyway, it's a pretty long way from Little Dear's house across the city to Stanley's outlying suburb near the university, and Barry won't drive himself since he does not countenance large cities. So Stanley and Olive see him just once at dinner, and Stanley tells Little Dear he'll go with her to take Barry to the train station for the trip home.

"Of course I will go by train," he says, the strike settled. "I never fly. I like to keep my feet on the ground."

While Stanley might be called by some on the short side, though he considers himself of medium height, and his sister is the same, their brother Barry is over six feet tall, and large. In fact, to several smaller races he has traveled among, say the Maya, he might be considered massive, looming tall and rounding out at about 250 pounds. His head sits on his body like a rotating globe, as Barry is very curious but also a priori certain as to what he sees and wants to see and thinks he sees. His feet are a notable feature in their length and size. As he was growing up, and up, his amazed father was often inclined, in affection and jest, his humor being broadstroke, to call Barry "Feet."

Now, the English professor beloved of his mostly first generation college students, Barry continues in his love for Smollett, Dickens, Thackeray, Trollope, and Dr. Samuel Johnson, often falling into one or another of these roles, becoming Dr. Johnson himself, or rubbing his hands together like Uriah Heep, or, down the scale, becoming Laughton doing Captain Bligh, or, on down, Oliver Hardy appealing for a little sense from his friend Stanley, as these favorite characters pop into his head. Barry Morris is one who relishes the academic's latitude for eccentricity and apparent carelessness in the face of society's conventions—though it is a pose. (As, he contends, is his brother Stanley's occasional pose as the Stoic philosopher Marcus Aurelius.)

This August morning Barry is clad in rumpled shorts which cling to his legs like flags to the top of the mast, rumpled shirt soaked with sweat, and a gimme cap with no legend on it, dressed for comfort in his travel.

Little Dear parks her blue Bronco on the asphalt lot adjoining the train depot. Skyscrapers and freeways stretch away on all sides of them. Jets are silver specks in the brassy sky above. "Little Dear" was her nickname from their father. (He usually just called Stanley "Stanley," only in odd moments offhandedly calling him "Bud" or "Bub" when, to Stanley's mind, he couldn't quite seem to remember that he had given him his own name, "Stanley.") Similar to but different from the irony of "Feet," this appellation became humorous as Little Dear gained her size and athletic prowess. Her name is Margaret and now she rolls her eyes as her brother Barry opens the front passenger door and gets out, saying to them, "Thanks. See you next time."

Without waiting for her, he opens the back of the vehicle and wrenches his luggage out.

"Why," says Little Dear, sounding aggrieved as their father often used to sound, "we meant to wait with you for your train. You have more than an hour to wait."

"We'll walk you in, anyway," says Stanley.

"Suit yourself." Barry hoists his bags and takes off, limping, from the parking lot towards the station building.

Following him, Stanley takes Little Dear's arm, barely keeping her from running after Barry. The legend on her T-shirt says *Tuff Muthas*, which is the name of the soccer team she plays on, women from about age thirty on up to more than forty. To make up for their age disadvantage their strategy is to run out on the field right at first and knock down all the members of the other team. This in fact does earn the other teams' attention and respect.

"See, I told you," she says. "He's limping."

She is terribly concerned about Barry. While staying at her house he has told her he has diabetes. Going barefoot he has left bloody footprints on her kitchen linoleum. Apologizing, he says he doesn't realize it. Often there is no feeling in his feet.

"What is he doing? Oh God, where is he going?" she says.

Their large lumbering brother has entered the station but now veers away from the main concourse path and heads into a tunnel walkway to one side.

"Looks like he's going out to the tracks," says Stanley.

"My God!" says Little Dear. "Damned if he isn't."

As they come back out of the dark cool hallway into the blinding bright glare outside, Barry stands exposed to sun and baking heat and a fair wind on the platform, bags at his feet, swabbing his neck with a bandanna and looking at them with his wry curl of lip.

"Aha, Boswell!" he bellows at his brother as Stanley comes up to him. "Some horrible prairie that you live on, Sir!"

Little Dear walks to the end of the platform, contemplates the horizon, and comes back, walking impatiently, like a player who's been carded. There are no trains at this or the other two platforms. There are no other people on the platforms. "This isn't the right place to wait," she says. "Aren't you supposed to wait inside? Don't they have a waiting room or something, Stanley?"

Stanley shrugs. How people come and go on trains these days is beyond his ken.

"This is exactly where we are supposed to wait," Barry barks. "This is where the trains arrive and depart, and stay betweentimes."

They stand there for about twenty minutes in the broiling sun. Little Dear has not brought her sunhat and is turning red. Stanley's shirt is plastered to him. He has not had much of a chance to talk to Barry this visit, but he can't think of much of anything to say now. Usually they talk about the arguments for and against tenure and their faculty senates' respective new policies on sexual harassment and nepotism, or which of them has the toughest teaching load, but all that doesn't seem appropriate platform chat.

"So, have you finally read the last volume of *A Dance to the Music of Time?*" Barry says, peering down at him, arms behind him, much in the attitude of Bligh inquiring whether Mr. Christian has stolen his coconuts.

"Yes. A year ago. Polished off the twelfth one, got through the series. Why do you ask?"

"I was trying to think of something light and irrelevant enough for you to have read it."

Stanley laughs. This is Barry at his best. Barry in his own reading goes between heavy cryptic tomes and his old English favorites while—true enough—Stanley keeps among his favorites high soap opera like Anthony Powell's. It reminds him of his life.

"This is ridiculous!" croaks Little Dear, sounding like their father again, and marches towards the entrance back into the station.

"Come on," Stanley says to Barry. Barry shrugs and picks up his bags and limps along inside with Stanley where, sure enough, there is a waiting area for the passengers of departing trains. Barry's train will be three hours late.

"What the hell is this about diabetes?" Stanley says just before they leave him there to wait for the Philadelphia Eagle. "You're bleeding from the feet? Are you taking medication? Weren't you drinking bourbon at dinner? Aren't you on a diet?"

"Thought at first it was the goddamn gout," Barry confides. "Boy, was I relieved!"

That Sunday night in the hospital Stanley dreams of his father, so stern and strong until his own debilitating illness, who was so aghast at his sons both becoming professors instead of doing something more useful and profitable. Wonders in the anxious subtext of his dreaming what he and Barry can, will, do now, with parts removed. If they will be "strong at the broken places." Sits beside Barry looking out the window of the train as boys, as men, as life rushes so terribly swiftly by.

CHAPTER

7

"I'LL BE OUT OF here in a couple of days. Then I'll be holed up at home for about a month, I guess. The doctor says the main thing is not to push it. That the ones who have the problems are the ones who jump right up and play Strong Man. Like this fellow Jack Bompers, you know? The dean who went to Virginia? He called here yesterday to see how I was doing. Said he made a big mistake, jumped up and took out his catheter too soon, and now he barely makes it on his schedule, teaching, meetings, until about two o'clock, when he has to go home and just collapses. No energy and can't control his bladder either. So, boy, am I ever going to take it easy. I'll be the longest recovery son of a gun in history. Hell, I'll make the Prostate Recovery Hall of Fame.

"I hope I can take over the afternoon seminar, though, take it back from you in a couple of weeks. I don't see why they can't come over to the house like they usually do, and I can sit and nod and listen to them in the circle as I usually do while they read their papers. I should be able to do that. God, I hope I can. That will bring me sanity and salvation, if I can do that by then, I'll tell you.

"So how's it going with you, Joe? I'm sure the classes are going well. I can't tell you how much it means to me for you to take them over for me."

"They're OK, I guess, Professor Morris." Try as he does, Stanley cannot get Joe Green, his best and favorite graduate student, to call him "Stanley." Joe is a New Age guy, loves the form of things and is natural as can be, but always respectful, formal with him. He is fascinated with the correspondence of literature and film, so Stanley has let him take the course in that direction; and the kids are also writing stories, screenplays, doing creative stuff between the genres.

"I don't know," Joe says. "Teaching seems so damn hard. You do it so easily—"

"Whoops—I do? Oh, my."

"Yeah. I either overdo it or I'm too loose and nothing happens. You know? I really work hard on this lesson, so I'm sitting there lecturing like I hate to be lectured to, and then I stop, and it's real Bomb time, they don't even have expressions on their faces. Or I'll just play like I'm one of them and here's a real interesting idea, like you do sometimes, and open up the floor and then the same two or three dweebs take the ball and toss it back and forth and the others let them do it. I don't know, Professor Morris, all the time I'm in class trying to be an interesting teacher I'm thinking, really, about my music, and then I go home and dig out my poor pitiful dissertation and read it and decide it's a piece of shit. I don't know. I mean, it's a hard profession, this teaching. I mean, I really knew what I was doing, working that cemetery."

Joe is a whiz at landscaping, grass, bushes, flowers, shrubs, laying it all out, and has been keeping Stanley's yard for him lately. Even before the operation he would appear and get the Craftsman mower out of the garage and mow the front and back and never take a nickel, saying, "Oh, I like to mow. You know? I miss it. Thanks for letting me do it."

Now he says, "I talked to Harry Connick, Jr., in New Orleans. Did I tell you that I knew him in those days?" Joe is older than the usual beginning grad student, though they are of course all ages now. "I tell him what a great teacher I am, and he laughs. He's cool. He was encouraging me to come back, play some music."

"I was your age, oh probably four or five years younger, when I walked into the first freshman English class they gave me," Stanley says. "'My God, is that the teacher?' one of the students said. He was a veteran, had dog tags around his neck, or I imagined he did. We still keep in touch, old Charley Duffey, he's in California now. My voice cracked when I began to speak to that first class. My first student evaluations said I stood and looked out the window a lot wondering what to say. It was the truth. I still get scared and halfway sick before each new class every term. No, I do. It's never easy. It can't be, if you care. I know you have your music, Joe, hell, you always will. But it seems to me you are a teacher."

Joe smiles. He's a rangy kind of corny-looking guy with, usually, bright happy eyes. He likes the kids he teaches, especially the first-year students who are kind of on the edge. It would be terrible to let Joe drift away from teaching, to let him leave.

Terrible for the yard, Olive says.

———

Gaining strength, walking regularly up and down the hospital hall, observing the bedded patients in the rooms along the way, his room looking more pleasant and reasonable to him, the tall orchid and the potted plants and cards in the window bay familiar now, mostly not reading and eschewing television, Stanley reflects on this and that, on his life past and his life to come, and so on, and comes to reflect again on the strange incident he suffered in the mountains the summer before and on the even stranger incident of the detection and removal of his malignant chestnut.

It's the July past. Time of bright mornings, the blooming of the pink-white saltcedar blossoms along the *ríos* and of clouded, thundery afternoons and sudden titanic evening thunderstorms in the mountains of northern New Mexico, where Stanley has gone to teach a month-long creative writing course at his university's forest-surrounded campus, the rebuilt cantonment called Fort Godwin.

Stanley rolls in in a rented car. Olive will join him in a week or two. He is greeted by the Fort director and by Rollie, the geologist and hiking enthusiast, and others on duty as faculty at the Fort. Most of Stanley's class are students he's taught before at the main campus. He feels he may be able to relax, maybe even write one or two of his secret poems this time while teaching this small, familiar class.

"What's up?" he says to Roberts, the anthropologist who has been director here for many years.

"Just the usual. The Indians are claiming—quite right, too—all the land along the edge of town where the best restaurants are, and all the air space above, and all the water rights in the county. Water's still up pretty good. Big snowcap been melting down. Hell of a storm, real one, two nights ago. Some of the Rainbow people came through and went to the casitas and tried to trade the students marijuana for beer, got mad because they wouldn't do it. Two kids thought they saw Captain Godwin walking the ridge again last night."

"Ho, ho," says Stanley, not doubting it a bit.

He walks by Polo. Polo is pretty long in the tooth by now. He is standing by the gravel road rubbing his wounded hand, watching their equally old friend Fortuno run the old Ford tractor culling the weeds and grass along the edges of the fort roads.

"Hey, Polo," Stanley says.

"Hey, Stanley," Polo waves. "You know that damn Roberts," he calls, "he's crazy as hell, man? I'll tell you later what he thinks he's gonna do around here. How's the old hen?"

Stanley motions that she's fine.

He takes a walk along the old nature trail. Everything is gold and dark and lighter green. A lot of pollen is in the air. He keeps sneezing and his eyes begin to run. Near where the *río* forks, where the swimming hole used to be twenty years ago, Stanley climbs up by a path in the thick pine, piñon, and cedar forest and goes by the battered remains of a treehouse his students built years ago and through the gold-green, waist-high meadow and around the ring of trees and back to the copse by the river. He stands and regards the plank remains of the desk he used to sit at here, conferring with students, reading their stuff, listening to the water sound, his little forest "office."

Then he goes up higher, up near the top of the ridge and to the old kiva where he and the best of the kids would come from time to time year to year and sit and contemplate the snowcapped peaks off in the distance, and the sherds lying around the ancient kiva walls, and this ancient culture, and the beauty of the clouds and trees, and the faded but still present past and the urgent present as students and teachers ever have been wont to contemplate in such an ageless setting.

On the way down, farther up the ridge, Stanley looks and thinks he sees Captain Godwin, in his blue Dragoon uniform and cap and chestnut beard, standing watching him below. He thinks he sees him wave though it is heavy twilight and it's probably just Rollie in his blue cap and sweatshirt and backpack up there on the ridge; but Stanley smiles. He likes to think it might be young Captain Godwin, looking down over, taking care of, his responsibility.

He goes back to his casita, by which the little *río* flows, sits on his portal and has a large toddy, then another. The altitude and the whiskey bring him peace, or wipe him out, as the case may be, and he skips dinner and hits the sack.

When he wakes in the morning his good eye is swollen and stuck shut. The other one gives him only a blur of vision. He goes to his first class hopeful that the eye will open and it will be all right. He sets the students to working on their stories.

A few days later, after many hot washrags to the eye, the eye opens and he sees a slightly better blur from it than from the other eye, but he can't read. What the hell, Stanley thinks, it will come back, at least he can see the shapes of his students. He doesn't mention this to Olive when he talks to her by phone.

He thinks maybe he should see a doctor, since it is his only useful eye. He finds a local doctor who assures him, though this is not her specialty, she is no ophthalmologist, that it's just a little tear on the eye and it will be OK with time. She of course has no more sense of what she's looking at than a goose, but he chooses to believe her because he does not wish to pull out and go home and because at this point he still believes intrinsically that nothing really bad or serious is due to happen in the measured life of Stanley Morris. Also because Olive is packed up and on her way for a little R&R. So he teaches on, legally of course blind.

Later on, it turns out it is not a tear but that the pollen has closed his eye and when it opened the lid has peeled off a layer of the eye. It turns out that discretion may have been the better part of valor, as far as healing goes. But Stanley doesn't know that. To him the print seems a little less fuzzy each day. He plugs along. It is not until Olive arrives and has her reaction that he admits how stupid he may be being. But he lies a little and says he is beginning to make out letters on the page, and Olive doesn't push to return home and see about it. She lets him plug on. She is married to a grown man who is perfectly capable of knowing the condition of his own eye, isn't she?

As for Stanley, teaching semiblind, not being able to read the students' stories, having them come to the casita and sit and read to him, he enjoys himself more than he ever has. The kids love it, reading their stories to him. He sits behind his dark glasses nodding like the Sphinx, full of wisdom as Bobbie or Wild Willy or Henry or Amanda reads. This way he is not critiquing them, going to the negative from the first, but listening, participating. He tells himself that this way he is actually helping them in the writing of the stories. They are being interactive in a purely human net or web. He tells himself this is terrific, a really cool thing to happen: if he ever did go blind, if something ever really happened to his eye, he would not have to retire. Old Professor Morris could go on teaching forever, blind—or until he got truly senile—and who would ever notice, as he sat smiling, nodding, listening to the students' stories?

Whether or not inspired by his blindness (and consequent lack of criticism), it is an enthusiastic class.

Bobbie Yuan, the Chinese-American girl, writes a story about not being accepted by a mainline sorority, and it's their bad luck. Wild Willy, actually a monster boy whose parents have brought him over from Northern Ireland, writes, of course, of Ireland. He has a lot of good stuff but doesn't quite know how to use it yet, so he ends all his stories with bad jokes and puns. Have you heard the one about the American-born priest from Boston who goes over to dear old Belfast—and—and stumbles into—er, sure—into a ring of Muslim terrorists? Well, sir, naow y' have.

Ozzie, the boy genius, writes a many-page story of a jazz musician's mad flight down into Mexico, into mescal, music and mysterious women. An older guy, Uncle Ed Harmon, writes some pretty outrageous "Return of Elvis" and "Spirit of Elvis" stories, not to mention his road classic of the trucker married to the Magician of Big Hair beauty parlor proprietress and her amazing large-scale holiday styling techniques.

But the master enthusiast of this group is a young man just back from a year misspent in Paris and so getting in shape by climbing a mountain daily. He is called "Q-Man" in reference to his constantly and loudly spoken enthusiastic use of a private vocabulary of positive epithets ranging from "Excellent!" to "Golden!" and culminating in "Quality!"

"Quality, man! Quality!" he explodes after almost every story read to the class aloud by its proud author. (He is not enthusiastic about Ozzie's jazz musician story. The dudes are going too far down into Mexico. It does not seem to him that they are ever going to get back, and the main thing always, man, is to get back.)

Q-Man is a sturdy guy with blazing eyes and muscles and great legs for climbing. Bobbie Yuan admires his legs but won't go climbing with him. Q-Man explains to Stanley, his Absolutely Quality Prof, that this is something definitely kind of Chinese having to do with upsetting the spirits up there on the mountain. Or maybe it's about not violating the space of Native Americans, Bobbie Yuan has been really into that. Anyway, she won't go up with him, so he has to settle for going with Wild Willy, who tends to drink at night, and who spazzes going up and kind of rolls and bounces back down the mountain but always makes it, man, because he has a romantic yet steadfast Irish heart, and is Quality.

They have a final class reading of stories starting at noon of the final day. Everyone reads his or her story aloud. Even Stanley reads one poem that he has written here this month while blind. Actually, he speaks it. He can see shapes and forms all right, and lights and colors, he just can't see to read. They all listen to the poem with respect, knowing he has not been able to write a story. It is a gnomic poem personifying the cedars of these mountains as tribal elders, whispering to you something you should know.

"That is lovely," says the kind young Chinese woman.

"That's mystical, man," says Ozzie.

"Quality," says Q-Man, prepping himself for his reading yet to come.

"The little trees come alive, like, and speak," says Freddie, Stanley's least favorite, who has written his story about a homeless guy who used to be a real estate broker.

"No shit they do," says Wild Willy. "Simple poem, but deep." He says "dape." "I talk to the feathery little bastards all the toime. G'me back me bottle, where'd y' 'ide it, I says to them, says I."

Stanley is embarrassed, oh a bit, about the poem but is somehow glad he shared it.

Reflecting on it now, lying in this hospital bed recovering from the surgery, Stanley thinks that this short bout of blindness, this small swerve from the normal routine, method and way of doing, was a sort of test as well as a premonition of debility that men face at his age; a signal if not a test; saying, this is John the Baptist, Stanley kid—the Big Boy's on his way.

Q-Man's story is about fifty pages long. It takes him a long time to read it aloud. He comes at the end of the lineup. He has invited friends from the other classes to come and hear it. Q-Man reads it with great flair and enthusiasm.

Q-Man's story is about some frivolous young people who come out to a place like this in some future time and get converted to Environmentalism, in which saving the natural beauty is Golden. The main young man and the main young woman join the subversive radical Underground which exists here (and always will). Their mission is to go up the highest Mountain in their sleek black Envirosuits and blow up the secret base of the wicked Government which is doing something evil Stanley does not quite understand related to the natural environment. Meanwhile the Government is limiting most personal freedoms, like not letting individuals go up the mountain trails, which are barred to citizens. Our heritage, the part of us that is Wild, is being denied to us.

"Blow the buggers bloody oop!" shouts Wild Willy from the back row. He has read a story about a young Protestant man who goes back to Belfast when his favorite aunt is blown up by a Catholic bomb. It is the first fluttering of the real wings of his talent.

Actually, Q-Man's main characters, first one, then the other, get killed by the Government, too. It's a funny story for the jolly positive Q-Man to write. It has essentially two parts that might be labeled "Youth" and "Death." In "Youth" it's talented, beautiful young people like Q-Man, Ozzie, Bobbie and Wild Willy reveling in, creating the world, making up and using their own language. "Death" is a symbolic picture of a grim controlled future with the essential stuff of life prohibited.

"Bummer, man," says Ozzie.

"No," shouts Willy. "Quality!"

"It makes me cry," says Bobbie Yuan, wiping tears.

Q-Man is down in spirit by the end because most of his friends, the students from the anthropology and biology and art classes, have left before he finished the story. Suddenly he brightens.

"Let's go climb the Big One!" he says.

"Golden!" says Wild Willy.

"You're out of your mind," says Ozzie.

"Aren't you worried about this guy?" says wormy little Freddie. "He's bipolar. Don't you think he should be committed, Dr. Stanley?"

"Morris," Stanley says. "It's Dr. Morris, to you."

"Come on, Professor, come with us!" says Q-Man.

"I don't think so," says Stanley. "You know, what with the storms we've been having, I don't think you should go up now, either. I think it's too late in the day."

Q-Man smiles at him as if he is the wisest, noblest Prof in the world, pats him on the back as if he is the child and he, Larry the Q-Man, the adult, and turns to Bobbie Yuan, who has consistently said no, who has never climbed, who, as Olive says, doesn't even have hiking shoes.

She smiles at the Q-Man and says, yes, she'll go.

Stanley is worried but thinks he can't forbid them; young as they are they are also "of age."

"You should have forbid them, Stanley," Roberts says, his gnarled face alarmed. "Are you losing your grip? How long have they been gone?"

"A couple hours by now." It has become late afternoon.

"Well, we'll call the ranger station, try to keep track of the weather. Where's Rollie?"

"He's probably in his casita, probably by now he's drunk," says Polo. "You know that damn Rollie, eh? We find them vodka bottles in his trashcan every week."

"Bullshit," Roberts says. "Tell him to get his climbing gear together."

"You tell him, you think you the *jefe* of the world. I'm not gon' tell nobody nothing except go tell my damn old cow time to come on home. You hear that cowbell ding-a-ling you know it's in honor your damn retirement, *que va!*"

"I'll tell him," Stanley says.

"Hey, Stanley," Polo says. "Don't worry about them damn kids.

Hell, they can do anything, you know? Well, I don't know. You see them black clouds? Way over there? There's gonna be a big storm on that mountain, looks like."

Stanley and Roberts ride with Rollie in his dusty pickup to the takeoff point of the trail. The sky is black, as well as Stanley can see it, but there is no storm down here. But you can see lightning flashing around the mountaintop. Lightning can splinter a tree or a person up there in a storm in an instant. It is terribly dangerous.

"Hell," says Rollie. With rope and pack and first aid stuff he starts up.

"Smoke?" says Roberts, sitting by Stanley in the cab of the truck. Stanley takes one. He has not smoked in years. He lights the cigarette, inhales, goes quite woozy, nearly swoons from the unfamiliar smoke in his lungs up here at eight thousand feet.

Later, what seems hours, it darkens, then is dark.

They sit at the foot of the trail in the truck with its lights on. Beside them is parked Q-Man's BMW.

They hear a noise, like a shout or a long halloo. It's raining, thundering, down here now. Then: "Hol-ee shee-it! Holee Shaat! Hoooly—"

Wild Willy comes yelling, tumbling down the trail, collapses in a heap before them.

"Where are they? Where's Bobbie, for God's sake?"

"Where in the bloody—thundrin'—hell—do y' think she is?" he heaves.

And here comes, in a moment, running and leaping along in tennis shoes and shorts and somebody's flapping old army jacket on her little form, Bobbie Yuan, running down the mountain from the thunder and the lightning and the pouring rain.

"I wasn't sure I knew the way. I couldn't see," she gasps. "I heard you shouting—"

"What you think I was a-shaouting for?" says Willy.

And bursting down, blood streaming from one leg, into the carlights and the flash beams, his hair plastered, comes Q-Man. Runs up and puts his arms around Bobbie Y.

"I was right behind you. I would not have left you up there."

"He pushed me, turned me around, I think he kicked me," Bobbie says. "He said to run like hell. Boy, am I telling you, I did!"

"Bloody lightnin'," says Willy. "Get your boons toasted up there, for sure, eh?"

"Oh boy! My God!" says Q-Man. "Wasn't that the greatest, running down? Oh, superb! Oh, Golden!"

"Quality!" they all say together. The kids, the Q-Man and Willy and the slight but sturdy girl.

Just then Rollie the expert climber comes ambling down. "Quality, my rear," he says.

"Where you been?" says Roberts.

"I just ducked to the side. Just got out of the way." Rollie starts to laugh, as the kids roll off in Q-Man's Beamer. "I don't believe I have ever seen anything, animal or human, come down off that mountain at that rate of speed! Funny thing though, I swear there was someone else up there. Maybe it was Captain Godwin, you think so, Stanley?"

Stanley stands in the rain a moment as Rollie and Roberts get in the truck. He beams his flash back up the trail. Up a way and slightly off the trail his beam finds Polo. He is in a pointed hat and a slicker and has a pointed staff in his hand. Stanley feels he is seeing an Hispanic image of two or three hundred years ago, a sudden surreal

Velázquez etched by his flash for a moment in the rain and darkness. The figure makes no move or signal and Stanley switches off the beam.

Oh my dear children, Stanley thinks, now yet more reduced, lying recovering in this hospital, *I sat there helpless. What could I do for you? What could I do for you? Oh my children, my students, my life . . .*

CHAPTER

8

STANLEY IS GOING HOME. He looks outside to a clear day, envisions
the route home, sees Olive readying the house for him.

He sees her making up the bed that was their daughter's when
she was home in her bedroom next to the master bedroom upstairs
in the old house. This will be Stanley's room for a while now. On the
other side of it is the small room that serves as his study, with his special books in bookcases on the wall, his Bombay desk, a small extra
bed for company, a constant litter of loose books and student papers
to read and grade and endless reports of the committees that Olive
opines keep the university moving while going around and around
in many different directions instead of going somewhere in particular. This, he knows she thinks, is what he so loves about the university, "his" university and sometimes the one that really exists, its
endless studies, its ideals for education, its structure, its protocol, its
terms, its beginnings and its endings, its *tabula rasa*, as Stanley says,
underwritten with its form, its conventions, its dedicated truths, all
scribbled on the board, as Olive sees 'em, in hieroglyphics.

And she is right. Olive knows him well, the Stanley who sees himself as a free and liberal thinker, who has played a hand or been a voice in intellectual, creative and social issues of their time as they have come at him, but who in his bones is a deep and true conservative.

She makes the bed fresh and welcoming. There will be enough plump pillows, and the slim one for the neck, for him to sit up and read by and to sleep on. She will know to put some biography and lighter stuff on the bed stand for him to read at first. He has not been able to read much of anything, even the newspaper, in the hospital. Olive works the *New York Times* crossword, but Stanley dislikes crosswords. He knows it perplexes her. Why would a man whose life is devoted to language not like crossword puzzles? Because it's a game, he tells her, you learn the codes, especially the little fill-in words, and you've got it, it's no real use of the mind at all. She tells him that as usual for him, he's somewhat wrong and somewhat right. She can see what he means, but she likes to work the puzzles, to figure out the words, go across first and then down, never both at once, to lance the word and have it fit. She likes to solve the puzzle and look at the answer the next day and see if she is right, and she likes to go on to the next one. The real reason Stanley doesn't like working crosswords, as she knows, is that she is quicker at it than he is. He likes it fine when he gets hold of an easy one, she tells him, like on the airplane. She's observed his little trick of working one going and then working it again with the speed of light on the return trip, knowing all the words, just to make himself feel good, or to impress the person sitting next to him by how fast he fills it in. She's on to him. Probably she won't put anything to read by the bed, knowing that as he can he'll poke around in the books in the room, just picking them up and hefting them, so soothing, and then prop himself up in bed dipping into old Thoreau or *Pickwick Papers* one more time.

"As does my brother Barry," he'll say, "I do love Mr. Pickwick and Sam Weller and Tupman and Snodgrass. I think what we like about Pickwick is that he is 'a good man,' as Dickens keeps telling us. I think it is amazing for a writer at so young an age to have created something so rare as 'a good man.'"

And she'll nod as if she's never heard it before, in her fourth decade of being married to him, and, he hopes and believes, think that he's a pretty damn good man himself.

There is a mirror in the upstairs hallway. She usually pauses to look in it. Her eyes are like emeralds. He hopes they are not clouded now. He beams his thoughts to her, that he is all right. (Every indication, dear God, is that they got it all . . .) Their life will go on. He will not be an old—dribbling—impotent—squiggly fellow—

He needs her faith. He knows she will have no doubt. She has not built a life with him on the basis of any doubt. She has a religious faith that leads her always to good works, and her faith in life and in their life and in herself and, he knows, in Stanley goes deep. Since he came home and told her and she had a vodka straight and he had a stiff Scotch or two and she cooked filets their life together has been a walking prayer. Her faith grounds them. It will greet him as he comes in the front door of their old house, he and dear "Priscilla."

Last evening she sat in here by his hospital bed and they talked about it. Olive's mother has had cancer and is sailing right along, but Olive doesn't know much about cancer in men. Stanley's colleague

Berton Benbow, in Philosophy, died last year after his prostate operation didn't get it all. Went so quickly. Stanley went to Benbow's memorial service and came back depressed. Now he figures from what he's heard there must be a dozen other prostate cases, in the active faculty or *emeriti*. His friend in the English department Si McGee had stomach cancer years ago and is doing well, teaching strong near retirement, sipping a little wine and beer.

Then there is Dean Bompers. He stays on Stanley's mind and bothers him, since Bompers's case is most like Stanley's and he does not seem to be doing so well. It bothers Olive that this worries Stanley.

"So what kind of a dean was Bompers?" she asks him. "Authoritarian," he replies. "Too quick to judgment, awfully tough on himself and others."

"Well," she says, "Bompers is Bompers. He's not you. For pity's sake, don't compare yourself with Jack Bompers. I am sure you will take the longest time to recuperate of anyone who ever had prostate surgery. You will be fine."

"Well, actually he was a pretty good dean."

"Which you aren't. You aren't even dean material."

"Oh? I was nominated."

"You were nominated by your dear friend Inder Singh. I think it was a joke."

"No. Inder doesn't joke. He was sincere. He said that since I am the chief faculty toady to the dean I might as well be dean."

"I see. Yes. That is much more flattering. Anyway, the Bompers type you're not."

"No," he says, adjusting the bed. "I am a great, measured Stoic philosopher. Apparent apathy. Etcetera. Would you please adjust these pillows? I can't get them fixed right behind my back. God, I'm so tired of this bed!"

Olive reflects that she doesn't know other wives whose men have had cancer. She has no friends whose husbands have the prostate kind. Well, there is Natalie, old Bob Kettle's wife, who will tell you the long nine-year horror of Bob's diagnosis for prostate cancer and his opting for not treating it—his impotence—the terrible pain that came to him finally—his death in the tenth year of horrible purgatory . . .

"Swell," says Stanley.

"You made a different choice. You dealt with it." She looks at him. Her emerald eyes blaze and say: Dr. Miller's strong hands reached in and got it and threw the damn insidious thing away!

Sitting there side by side the evening before his homecoming day they pray silently together, that their privileged, positive life will continue as before, Stanley's in his university and with her, hers with him and in her little shop she goes to daily that is not exactly her refuge but is another world just as real as Stanley's—or more so—and is her counterbalance to all the weight of the machinations of the university which Stanley brings home to share each evening.

They talk, for a moment, then, about the possible after-effects, even of the damnable thing coming back. They do not talk about—the other. Dr. Miller says they saved the veins, so he shouldn't be impotent. That is enough for now.

As she gets up to go Olive laughs, out of the blue.

Now, he knows, everything will be clean and in place and ready, upstairs and downstairs in their "mansion." He beams at her to come on and get him. She'd said she would set up a bed and make a bedroom for him downstairs in the TV-den room, called him a hardhead for not agreeing. He is sure he can make it up the stairs even though the doctor isn't sure he should. He wants to be upstairs as he recovers, with his study nearby, so he can look out the window to the backyard, to their two great ash trees and to the old garage with all his tools in it and to the honeysuckled fence and the plot where every spring he plants his garden.

He gets up to don the robe and watch out the window for her.

CHAPTER

9

THE GOOD, KIND HARRIETT wheels him down from his room to the entrance of the hospital. He thanks her for all her good services. "You be good," she says.

As Olive comes to claim him from Harriett and he sits in the wheelchair at the hospital doorway he looks back into the lobby.

"Who are you looking at?" Olive says, taking the handles behind him and moving him towards the waiting car. "Who is that?"

"Oh," Stanley says. "Oh my."

It's Mack and his buddy Jesus sitting there on a couch in the lobby across the way from the lady in pink at the desk. Yes. Goodness. It's Jesus and Mack, both just in mufti like regular folks and sitting there together giving a wave to him, wishing him good luck and Godspeed as he leaves here and gets back to home and his life. That's nice, he thinks. He waves and says, or mutters, something.

"What?" says Olive.

Stanley laughs. What can he say? She'll think she's taking a nutcase home. For a moment, wheeling out her husband who seems to be waving and speaking to someone invisible, she kind of thinks she is.

Stanley is amazed, sitting in the front passenger's seat in his robe and slippers, as the car stops and starts and turns and merges and yields and stops at lights and goes along the roadways to their nest of familiar streets and houses in this city. Where do all these people come from? Where do they live? What in the world do they do? How do they make it?

"Am I mistaken, or are there a lot more Lexuses and Infinitis and Mercedes than there were a week ago?" he says.

"It's the Republicans," Olive says, "helping the economy."

They pull into their driveway and park by the Japanese tree that makes a bower of limbs and leaves in front of the bright red door of their old two-story house of stone and wood. Olive comes and opens the car door for him. He gets out, like a crab, and straightens and walks slowly around to the bluestone steps she has swept and slowly up them and, "Priscilla" in hand, through the door she holds open of their house.

She sees tears in Stanley's eyes as he passes her and goes into the living room.

He settles into his daughter's room upstairs.

The bed is a little longer than he is and about twice as wide. Barry could not fit on the bed. It is wider and softer than the damn apparatus bed in the hospital. It is softer than his and Olive's bed. He sinks into it gratefully. The tube from the catheter in his penis is long enough so it can reach comfortably to the urine bag on the floor beside the bed. From time to time during the day he will get up and take and empty it in the toilet of the bathroom across the way. That is his schedule, plus taking a few pills and eating meals, and drinking lots of cool tea and water. He feels no pain; the urine is clear and flows smoothly to the pouch. He does not even feel its flow. There are no surges or spasms. There is no feeling. Nothing that aches in him or even twinges. In the bed he is in a cocoon.

This is a time of isolation for Stanley, a time of almost perfect equilibrium. Even Olive, as she comes and goes, solicitous, bringing delicious, thoughtful meals and snacks up the stairs, then disappearing down below, going off to her little shop, leaving him alone, is more like a nurse, a visitor to his room, than like—Olive. He lies in the bed at peace. He hardly has a thought. It is a vacuum time. There seems to be little in his consciousness. It is like he always imagined the peace of Zen would be. He enjoys it.

If he were an anthropologist he could trace his daughter's life from being in this room.

The walls of the room are white. There is a flowered border between the wall and ceiling. The door is white. The sheets and pillows are white. The bookcases to the left and the desk and dresser to the right are white.

There are pictures around the room of her and other little girls at the camp she loved, and of high school and college times. Shakesbear and her other bears, usually on the bed, sit on the floor. Big Doll and some of her other early friends sit atop the bookcase. It is crammed with books from all her ages from Raggedy Ann to Mrs. Tittlemouse and Pooh to the Hobbit to Jane Eyre and Ernest Hemingway. Textbooks from her college courses and, my God! *Cliffs Notes* on *Merchant of Venice, Crime and Punishment,* and *Return of the Native.* He has to laugh: his own daughter using *Cliffs Notes*!

He remembers carrying her on his shoulders through the woods to Hardy's house in Higher Bockhampton. They bought three gilt leather Hardys there. She has them now. Like himself, she always loved Hardy, and the old Hem. (Ah, Stanley thinks: Belmonte.)

That is what in his first teaching days they used to teach the first-year students, the "freshmen," when he was a rookie in the university: *The Return of the Native,* how Hardy "loaded the dice against his characters," and Joseph Conrad's *Victory,* and Sinclair Lewis's *Arrowsmith,* and stories like "The Most Dangerous Game" and "The Double Dyed Deceiver" and "That Evening Sun." Dear Lord. What a gone and buried age.

He tries to read a little. Light stuff. A little Brendan Gill. A little Thurber. Benchley. He dips back into old Benchley's *After 1905, What?* What, indeed? He has a stack of books that people send. They look impressive on his daughter's dresser. Someone gives him Bill Moyers's book on healing and the mind. He looks at it. It looks interesting. He should probably read it: the interaction of mind and body in healing. It is heavy and he puts it on the stack.

At night he reads or lies awake with the light on, Olive asleep in the room beyond.

———

Joe Green wants to come and see him. He says no, he'll see him later, next week. Next week he'll go down the stairs.

All week Stanley lies in the soft bed in the white room and prays and reads and does not think about much of anything and sleeps a little at night and in the afternoon and pisses effortlessly through the tube into the bag and empties it religiously and on schedule sits and eats the food that Olive brings him.

"How are you doing?" he always used to ask the Colonel when he would go to visit him, so lonely and alone, in his small apartment in the retirement village after Flo had died and the Colonel had turned ninety years of age.

"I am sitting up and taking nourishment," the Colonel would reply, with his kind boy's smile.

Which was, of course, sufficient to the moment and the best of news.

CHAPTER
10

"PROFESSOR MORRIS," JOE GREEN says, in his role as yardman, having just done a last fall mowing and mulching, "those bees are still buzzing around back of the garage. Do you want me to shoot the juice to them? Pull down that honeysuckle on the garage? It's peeling pretty bad. We should probably paint it."

They are in the backyard. Stanley has come downstairs. He has never beheld such a beautiful sight as the colors and shine of wood and glass and the pictures on the walls of his living room and dining room. In his robe he has gotten in the car as Olive drove to the big new supermarket and has sat in the car and watched the people come out with their sacks of groceries. It was a thrill. He waved at them and smiled, and some even waved and smiled back and no one flipped him the bird or even scowled at him. He is wearing a small bag strapped to his leg. "Priscilla" is forever gone. It is like trading a DC3 for a Lear jet. The world is good. He is making Progress.

Stanley is actually dressed. He has on his jeans and old loose shirt and sneakers. He stands out in the large backyard with Joe, slightly stooped, bent over a little, as if he is afraid of standing up too straight, not sure of what strain the incision will bear. He looks over his natural domain.

Stanley's yard and grounds are ragged. They look terrible. The grass is patchy up towards the house. The bushes are laced with fallen branches. Leaves, unraked, are everywhere and beginning to lose their colors. The old garage is peeling paint on the sides and on the back. But the trees are lovely, Stanley thinks. He loves his two large ash trees closer to the house, the old and the fresh young pecan trees in back. Part of his fence is falling down; the high back hedge is mostly dead. Ah yes: his grand estate.

The bees.

They are still buzzing around back here, all right, end of September. What should he do? Poison them? Then rip the honeysuckle off so they might stay away next year?

"No, Joseph," he says. "I think not." He moves closer to them, so they are flying in little arcs around his head.

"Be careful," Joe says. He is fearful of the bees.

"I hardly think I want to harm them now. Any more than they want to harm me. You know, Joe, there is a history to it. This old place—the house, out here— Well, the bees were here when we came, oh, thirty years ago. They've never left. They seem to have—what?—an affinity for the place."

He tells young Joe Green the story of the bees.

After Olive and Stanley moved into the old cracked house built on shifting ground, more and more started coming into the house through the chimney and the walls. Blackened honey began to seep through the wall in the living room beside the fireplace. Finally it got to be an onslaught, a "galore" of bees. (Not dangerous, actually, not aggressive bees but gentle, honey-making bees. But a horde of them. More damn bees, finally, in the house than even Stanley could abide.)

They take off the wood siding above the stone base of the house. Inside they find 120 pounds of blackened honey between the outer and inner walls. They find a lot of bees.

They find a man who comes, like the Pied Piper, and takes the hive on a long pole, holding it aloft, and walks away with it with a million bees hived around it. They hope he has the Queen. Then and now Stanley realizes how ruthless it was, and regrets it, but it was necessary, he supposes he would do it yet again, they find a nice old man named O. T. Gunlock who is a master poisoner. They remove the honey and Mr. Gunlock poisons the bees that are still hanging around and, as he says, "I guaran-dang-well-tee you, Mr. Stanley, they won't be back again." He goes off to his village outside the city and dies of cancer soon thereafter, and of course the bees come back.

The old fellow they bought the house from tells Stanley they always had bees in the wall and coming in the house but not that bad, it didn't call for drastic measures, in their years of living here. And the people they bought the house from, why, yes, they had mentioned a little problem with your bees. As far back as Stanley's knowledge goes, bees had always been associated with the house.

And here they are, just a small dragoon guard of them, buzzing, whisking around the back of the old garage.

And still, each spring, from somewhere, for some reason, a

bunch of them come down the chimney and come to rest on the floor of the living room and den, and lie there and die. You just accept them and try not to step on them and when they die you sweep them up and take them out and sprinkle them like organic stuff upon the yard and bushes.

"Weird," says young Joe Green. "So you don't want to do anything about these here?" Sometimes Joe reverts to the patois of his farm background.

"No," says Stanley.

They turn. They are standing on the rectangular plot where Stanley plants his vegetable garden every year. All around stuck in the ground are the old bent wire cages for his Early Girls and Better Boys, his Beefsteaks, and his little cherries.

"Look there," Joe says. He laughs. A strange priestly-looking praying mantis makes its way across the ridge of soil and grass, a leftover from the platoon Stanley put there last year to guard his truck from bugs. "What are you going to put in in the spring?"

"I don't know. Don't know if I can dig it."

Joe puts his hand for a moment on Stanley's shoulder. "Hell, I'll dig it," he says. "Not that you won't be able to. We'll get a tiller, maybe. Eh? You know, I think we could double the size of it. You ever tried corn, or them big old long squashes? We used to have those things, be three or four feet long."

Stanley gets moisture in his eyes. He feels like he has a son. He keeps tearing up lately. It's just part of it, he knows. But he must stop this damn emotionalism.

Looking around, and back, he thinks of Mack, as he so often does, and of how their fathers and they worked so faithfully on the gardens and on their grape arbor and berry bushes all the summers growing up, and of their chickens, turkeys, dogs, and goats on their old farmlike places not two miles apart . . .

He tamps the emotion down again. He goes over to the big bush of yellow roses in the corner of the yard under which are buried the ashes of his mother, Flo, and communes with her a moment.

Going in, he feels a little weak, unsteady, takes Joe's arm.

He has to empty the damn little bag strapped to his leg. It isn't half big enough to accommodate all the piss that's in him.

Inside, Joe says again he can't seem to concentrate on his dissertation. Stanley says he understands, since Joe is teaching more than a full load, with his own two advanced classes added to Joe's two first-year composition sections. Stanley kicks himself. He should not have saddled Joe with so much. One or another of his colleagues could have taken one or both of his classes, though he is not quite sure who. In the department you have the Theorists, the Aestheticists, the New Historicists, the Writers, the old Freudians and Marxists, the Feminists, and Stanley. He thinks of himself as a kind of utility infielder-outfielder in the profession now, kind of like old Smoky Burgess at the end of his career.

But Joe. Joe says he is going to decide by Christmas whether to stay in the Ph.D. program and finish his dissertation or to go on down to New Orleans and try his music full-time again.

Stanley nods at him, sympathetic friend and tutor, mentor. He suggests that maybe such a big decision should not be made by Christmas. But it's Joe's decision.

Jesus Christ, Joe! he thinks.

———

Olive has been screening his calls.

"Maybe you'd better take this one," she says. "It's Jack Bompers in Charlottesville."

"Hel-lo, Stan-ley?" Bompers says. He speaks slowly and deeply, accentuating each syllable, almost as if he has a speech impediment. As a matter of fact, he must have a speech impediment. This has lent authority, if not majesty, to his pronouncements as dean.

"Hello, Jack? How are you, Jack? How are you getting along?"

"Stan-ley? How are you do-ing? How are you get-ting a-long?"

"Fine, Jack. Fine. It's been, what? Two weeks, I guess. Just taking it easy. Looks good so far. How about you, Jack?" Jack is about a month ahead of him.

"Oh— Not so good. Not so good— Oh. What? Celeste is talking to me. Yes. OK. Is your cath-e-ter out yet, Stan-ley?"

"No. No, it's not, Jack. Won't be for a while yet, I guess."

"Oh. Stanley's cath-e-ter is not out yet, Celeste. I took mine out— oh—when I came home— It was a ter-rible mis-take— Oh— Good-bye, Stan-ley— I will call again. Right now you are not rel-e-vant—"

"Well—" Stanley says as Jack hangs up.

"What was that about?" Olive says.

"Oh boy," he says. Maybe he can make an arrangement to leave his catheter in for the rest of his life. What if, when he takes it out— Oh boy. Oh hell.

"He shouldn't call you, if he's not doing well," Olive says.

"Give the guy a break!" For the first time Stanley flares at her. She looks almost glad, for a second, then a little bit hurt, then angry. Her green eyes get that glint of blue in them.

Then she relents. "Take it as a warning," she says. "Take it easy. Enjoy this time. Can you write a little bit on that piece on Emerson at Oxford? I think that is really interesting. I think the point about Jack Bompers is that he went back too quickly."

"Yes," Stanley says. But in his own mind he resolves to relieve Joe of the long afternoon class, to have it here at home next week.

The next call she lets him take is from a student, a reporter on the campus newspaper, Melissa Stuart. She wants to come interview him for the paper. She understands he has been at the university forever. They want to know how he's doing, what he thinks about what's going on. He has no idea what's going on, but he is flattered. He says she can come for an hour Thursday afternoon. The president of the Faculty Senate, Bobby Lee, a geologist, also calls and wants to come by. Stanley tells him to come over for a little while before the student, Melissa, comes on Thursday.

Lee has a beard that wisps down his chin and gray hair under an old slouch hat he wears in the house. He looks a little like a yak. He brings Stanley a gift of a bottle of The Famous Grouse Scotch whiskey from the executive committee of the senate.

"Thanks," says Stanley, receiving it. "I have given up drinking, but if I ever do drink again the first one will be from this bottle. What's going on? How goes the search for the new dean?"

"That search committee is acting like a damn Star Chamber, Morris. Even our own people on it won't communicate. Inder Singh says we should make a resolution in the senate that we won't accept anyone they come up with, since they are obviously toadies of the president. President Biggs is authoritarian, you know that? A tyrant is what he is."

"Resolution, smezolution," Stanley says. "You ever see a resolution do any good? How many pounds of resolutions do we have stored in the files?"

"Inder says it should be more like, you know, an ultimatum."

"If I'm Art Biggs, or anyone who's president, the only answer to an ultimatum is 'no.'"

"Inder Singh says that you yourself are—"

"I know," Stanley laughs. "Don't touch me," he says to Bobby Lee. "You'll get warts."

"Anyway, we hear there's a woman and a black on the list, so that's good, if true."

"One and the same?"

Lee tugs at his beard, cuts his yellow eyes to Stanley. "Probably not. We don't want to come out of the Ice Age too fast," he says as he departs.

"I am offended," Olive says, coming in from her listening post in the kitchen. "That character kept his hat on in my house!"

"That character is fairly famous. Spends most of his time in the desert."

"I know that. I know all about how famous and affected you guys are. Wearing your hat in the house is a silly affectation. Or else it's just plain assertive and rude. Was he raised in a barn? Does he think our house is a tent in the Sahara? Pooh, Stanley. Did he say the new dean might be a woman? Dear God, I think it would be the greatest thing in the world if you men, you bunch of affected characters, had a woman deaning over you!"

"We have quite a number of women on the faculty."

"Oh yeah? How many full professors? How many in your own department, Stanley?"

"Never mind," he says.

When Melissa Stuart arrives Stanley sees that she is black. She is beautiful and black, with large eyes and white teeth and small round glasses. In his robe, trusty bag neatly emptied and strapped tight, hair brushed back with fingers, Stanley greets her, courtly, at the door, ushers her in, sits on the couch in his living room as she sits in the old wing chair with pad and pen and recorder in hand.

"Do you mind if I record this?" she says, smiling, looking around, her gaze lingering at the books on the nearest shelf.

"Yes." He minds. He does not want it recorded for posterity.

She accepts his decision cheerfully. "They say you have been here forever, I mean, in the university," Melissa says. "They say you are part of the firmament."

"Or the pediment." Stanley smiles. This is a neat kid.

They talk about a lot of things. Stanley feels he is saying silly, obvious things like the liberal arts teach students to think and that the new perspective truly is that our world is a very small, fragile planet with a lot of people on it.

"You mean, like, global?" Melissa says.

"I mean, like, the Golden Rule, and empathy," Stanley finds himself saying.

Melissa nods. She knows it. At the end, as she sees he is tired, she says, "What brought you here, to Highland? Didn't you come here as a student and then come back, after you got your advanced—what?—to teach?"

"Yes," says Stanley. "Degree. I'm not sure how I got here—as a student. But once I got here, I loved it. Highland. Our good university. Well—"

Finally Melissa Stuart says, "I've been wanting to ask you since I came in—I can tell you were quite a dude, Professor Morris, I mean like in your day. I mean, I'm dying to ask you— What is the craziest thing you ever did?"

Stanley, dude, smiles. He beams at her. He shakes his head.

"I have never done anything crazy in my life," he says.

"Oh, man!" she says, flicking his arm, bobbing her head, as they stand up, rolling her eyes at him.

He sees her to the door.

"Seemed like a nice kid," Olive says. "How did it go?"

"Maybe they won't run it."

"Why in the world did you agree to give an interview right now? Oh well. Aren't half the girls now named Melissa?"

"Seems like," he says. He does not say he is in love with this one.

Olive drives him to the medical building where he first trudged along the halls taking his records in all innocence from dear jolly old Dr. Fishbein to Dr. Miller.

Stanley is in some terror as they drive. He keeps jamming his right foot on an imaginary brake. "Stanley!" Olive says.

He tries to settle down. Suddenly he grabs at the dashboard, making Olive swerve the car. A small car driven by an Asian man peering ahead, gripping the steering wheel, has turned in front of them.

"I thought he was going to hit us," Stanley says.

"Stanley . . ." Olive says.

Inside the medical building he is pleased to be walking along these halls on his own again. He gets some X-rays taken, gets some blood taken, then reenters the office, with its pictures of hunting dogs on the walls, of Dr. Miller, who first startled him so. Miller regards him, rolling the Mont Blanc pen in his hands.

"You're fine," he says. "I think we got it. Everything looks fine.

It was a little close to the edge there, but we'll follow your PSA along. It seems fine so far. Your PSA is zero-zero-a-little-something-one, I bet it will go zero. We'll keep track of it, see what's what as we go along. So, do you want a round of radiation?"

Radiation? Stanley is stunned. No one has mentioned radiation.

"Radiation? What for? If we—you, I mean—got it—"

"Just to make sure. It was pretty close to the edge, Professor. That's all. Some patients at this point like to make sure, take a round of radiation, just to wrap it up. Sometimes just to treat the trepidation, you know what I'm saying to you?"

"You think we got it all?"

"Yes, sir. I think we did."

"So, I don't have trepidation. I don't want any radiation."

"Good. You're my man. I like the way you make decisions. I don't see anything, now, so it's your decision to make. You know what I'm saying, Professor? If, later, the PSA tells us anything different— Well, we'll see what's what then, maybe make another decision, eh? Meanwhile.

"All right. Do you hunt or fish, Professor Morris?"

"Used to fish a little. Old cane pole on the lake. Never did hunt." Stanley has always hated hunting, and the idea of it, but now he feels bad telling this guy across the desk from him, this guy who has probably saved his life, he doesn't hunt.

"I enjoy it," Miller says. "Like to go out with my dogs and shoot. Like to find and shoot them—dove, quail, ducks, all the birds." His eyes go opaque. Stanley realizes he and Dr. Lester Miller will never really know each other, be friends. Well. He wishes there is something he could do for him but has no idea what in the world it might be.

"Good-bye, Professor," Dr. Miller says, taking Stanley's hand in his sharp strong grip, quickly releasing it. "Dr. Martz will remove your catheter, oh, let's not rush it, I want you to take it easy, you know, say in another week and a half, two weeks. All right? Miss Hish will make the appointment for you."

Miss Hish still has the large eyes like fish that swim in a bowl. He remembers Miss Hish, how she took the folder from him, how she ordered him to sit and wait for Dr. Miller to examine him. He wonders if she remembers that little changing point in his life. She writes the appointment in her book, looks up at him with her swimming eyes which seem to find him for a second, like they are locating something through water and glass. She smiles a weak, thin smile at him, pats her dull brown hair, goes back to her records and accounts.

"You are beautiful," Stanley says. He means it, for she had done more than receive his folder. She had detained him, led him in to Miller, sat at the fulcrum of his life.

He turns and goes out the door of the doctor's office with hunting tapestries on the walls, not looking back to see her reaction, if any.

Late at night, sleepless, Stanley goes downstairs and sits in the dark in the den. He can see the pale screen of the television set and the flashing of the number thing on the VCR, blue flashing numbers, that he is not smart enough to fix. The whole wall beside him is shelves of books. He will never get them all arranged properly. He has begun a list by various categories noting what are first editions and what are signed by the author. Pretty anal, eh?

He thinks of his little project on Emerson. The guy was always sick, depressed, people he cared about all dying around him, and he comes up shiny-bright with transcendentalism! But who cares about when Waldo was in Oxford, or what he did or thought there? It's just a little piece of something and Stanley can't seem to get hold of anything much bigger. He was only interested in it himself, really, when he was there some years ago, at the college in Oxford. He can think of a dozen scholars who are doing Emerson.

The last few days, when he is able to go up and down stairs, he has sat here afternoons, Olive at her shop, and watched old movies on the AMC, after which some corny old guy tells about the film and shows old publicity interviews of the stars. It makes Stanley laugh. He sees some dreadful old flicks, several about the French Foreign Legion, and enjoys them. He sees *Beau Geste* and *Gunga Din.* He sees *Forever Amber* and *Unconquered* and they remind him of high school days, when he and Mack double-dated with the successors to Ann and Debbie, Hedda and Marilyn. Two nights ago *For Whom the Bell Tolls* comes on late and he sits up, so excited to behold Robert Jordan and Maria and Pilar and Pablo again that he can hardly stand it. My God, he has forgotten: they had opening music, and an intermission, like *Gone with the Wind.*

They had the inscription of the great poem, of no man being an island, entire of itself.

True, but hell, every man is pretty much of a separate little isle, too, don't you think?

Stanley does. He has never felt more like an island.

He looks around. He almost sniffs, like an animal in its burrow. He feels that Mack, his brother Mack, is near. He feels that Mack has not shed, escaped, his troubles. He feels that somehow he might be able to help old Mack. Mack is still not at rest, he's in limbo, still running along that trail . . .

He falls asleep in his comfortable chair, then, thinking of his real brother, Barry. He wonders how Barry's stump is coming along. He wonders why Barry has not called. He gives a small laugh, knowing Barry wonders why he, Stanley, has not called . . .

When he wakes, stiff, he pulls himself up the stairway by the railing, hearing the old house creak and shudder in fall wind and rain, and for the first time goes and lies down by Olive on their bed. She sighs sweetly and says something in her sleep and puts her arm, sensing him there, upon his chest.

He turns to her, kisses her cheek, puts his hand upon her chest, feels her lovely breast. He feels deep contentment but nothing else—no twinge even in his catheterized part, no stirring of desire, not a murmur of the old dawning of the urge, the coiling up . . . He touches her cheek—she sighs—and turns upon his back again. He wonders, as he recites his prayer, if he will ever feel that twinge, that urge, again.

CHAPTER

11

STANLEY GETS OUT. HE takes a walk around the block.

It's a long block. Next door Ralph Winterhalter is in his back shed taking paint off the frame of the '58 Thunderbird he is restoring. On the other side Ed Bigelow, his semiretired neighbor, who is a little younger than Stanley, is sitting by his pool reading. On along, Byron Siwacki, who is seventy-five, is up on his roof cleaning out his gutters. Next to him old Ned Nettles, who is ninety-two, is viewing what's left of his summer garden. He has put a new grape arbor along the fence that won't do much for a few years yet. None of their neighbors actively works; except for Ed, they haven't for years. They all nod and wave; he doesn't know whether or not they know he has had surgery. They have accepted him as a suitable neighbor through the years because, as a professor, he doesn't seem to them to do much either.

He comes back into his own yard and stands by Flo's rosebush. It is holding on, a mellowed yellow. He forgets what star or personality the rosebush is named for. He sees two guys are standing up by the bigger ash tree. It is Mack and Jesus (the order of course should be Jesus and Mack) standing there in daylight, under the sun of a cool late September morning. He goes up to them.

Jesus stands back a little. He is really just kind of a force, or presence. He nods. He is a terrifically deep-looking guy. A couple of the bearded Jewish guys in Philosophy and Religious Studies look like Him. Somehow He communicates to Stanley so Stanley feels it deeply, that his mother Flo's spirit is free and well, that the Colonel's also is so, and his father's, that all are free of their burdens and are reconciled. Stanley minds his great-aunt Bertha, his grandfather's sister, who used to scare him when he was a small boy by saying she spoke to Jesus about him. He thinks of old Aunt Bertha humming "In the Garden."

Mack smiles at him. Thank God he does not wink.

"You seemed sad," he says. "I'm OK. I have just got to get through it."

"This is weird," says Stanley. "I mean, I'm supposed to be recovering."

"Oh, you're all right. Stan the Man. You're fine. What the hell, babe, you think spirits don't exist? Well. Is there anything you'd like to ask me, or Him?"

"Why?"

"Why'd I do it? Oh Stanley— But, if you mean this: There was nothing you could have done."

"I never thought—you would."

"And I guess you still, in your foolish Romantic heart, think you will live forever, don't you, Stanley? I remember you always thought, and would try to get us pepped up, every year in high school, that we would beat Blue Ash Township in football, too. Yo, Stanley. What a guy!"

Then: *"Got to go. Got to be on my way. I'll get there. Take it off your heart, Stanley. Live on as you can, in this strange world of appearances, my Brother."*

Jesus smiles, and fades. He seems as solid as the old ash tree, and fades into the atmosphere. And Mack nods solemnly, and fades away as well. Departs. It's as if he merges into Flo's bush of yellow roses—like the ballplayers in the movie who cross over into the cornfield and are gone.

Olive asks him how his walk was. He says it was a good experience, being out again. He does not tell her he has been in the company of angels.

Little Dear calls. She has been faithful checking on him. She has talked to their brother Barry, called him in New Jersey. Somehow Barry is managing to teach. He has crutches in the classroom and a wheelchair at home. He is looking forward soon now to having his prosthetic foot. She bawls him out for not checking on Stanley. Barry says he has been composing Stanley a long letter, in Old English, but he is a little rusty in Anglo-Saxon so it will take a while to complete. Stanley says it's just as well.

Melissa Stuart's story comes out in the campus newspaper, with a smiling picture of him from several years ago: CANCER CANNOT STOP PROFESSOR. It's a nice story, all about his long career in the university. It quotes Stanley as saying, "Whenever I walk on campus all fresh in the morning, I feel like I'm 21 years old again and just beginning to teach."

"You do?" says Olive.

The story quotes President O. Arthur Biggs as saying Stanley is very dedicated. It quotes his colleague Inder Singh as saying he is a nice person who earnestly tries to do the right thing though often blinded by his strange loyalty to the president and dean. It says that Stanley is a firmament and a pediment of the place, and he will return to campus the next week. It doesn't mention the craziest thing Stanley never did.

"Well," says Olive, looking at the headline, "if anyone on campus didn't know you had cancer, they know it now."

"Say," she says, "since you are getting so active, why don't you come help out at the shop? Rose and I need to go to the gift market downtown Thursday afternoon. You could just sit in the shop, and read, and keep it open for us. I doubt many people will come in. Business has been slow."

"I can't work the credit card machine."

"Good Lord, Stanley! It's easy. I've shown you how."

"I'd screw it up. I can't get the lever to work over the card."

"Well, that's OK. 'Take the cash and let the credit go.' It probably won't make a bit of difference."

Stanley has the long afternoon seminar at home. He tells Joe not to come. The kids all come in and sit around the living room. It goes pretty well. When he gets tired and runs out of gas talking about Willa Cather, they take over the discussion. Actually Stanley gets sentimental. He loves *My Antonia,* the story and the form of it, its clarity and strangeness and hidden women's depth, its American-ness. They have a long break for cookies and sodas, and he lets them go half an hour early.

But he does it. He is teaching again.

The next afternoon, Wednesday, O. Arthur Biggs wheels into their driveway in his elegant old black Mercedes for a brief visit. He wears a pinstriped suit that seems too heavy for the warmish day. The president has a sense of style which leadership demands. Stanley greets him in his university T-shirt, shorts, and sneakers. They stand rather formally in the living room, then Stanley invites him to come sit in the old comfortable chairs in the den.

"As you know," O. Arthur says, "I admire your library. I look forward to retiring, if I don't die first, so I can catalogue mine. I would like to semiretire, like you, and teach again, if I can beat the Grim Reaper to it. If I had legs like yours, Morris, I don't believe that I would go around in shorts."

"It's nice to see you, Art. I appreciate you coming by. I am feeling out of touch. What's all this Grim Reaper stuff?"

O. Arthur waves a pudgy hand. "Oh. Oh hell. I have had another flare-up of the ticker. I am going in for tests. I may have to take a leave of absence, Stanley. It is not good public relations to die in office. You know? It shakes the confidence of the donors and the alumni, maybe even the students. Would give 'em something to talk about at the Faculty Club, I suppose, eh, your buddies there? Actually, I went over and had lunch with that bunch the other day. Your pal Inder Singh and the so-called Table. Professor Singh informed me when I was floating names for this really damn important assignment that is coming up that you are a well-known toady to the president."

"I have been promoted," Stanley says. "I'm sorry to hear about your flare-up. You better not float my name, or think of me, for any new assignment. I'm getting there but I'm still a little shaky on my feet. What is it?"

"A new task force. We need a heavy faculty presence, on academic and human values, input on academic planning. Counterweight to all this reengineering the trustees are pushing. You know? Anyway, I wanted you to know the situation. Things are a wee bit precarious. They are likely to get precariouser."

"What will happen, if you have to take a leave of absence?"

"Herb Hesseltine."

"Oh my. Oh my goodness."

"Has to be. He takes over as acting president. It's in the bylaws. You know that."

"I hope you are OK, or get a lot better really quick."

O. Arthur laughs. "Yeah. It's enough to make you think about disregarding doctor's orders."

Herb Hesseltine is a pleasant duffer who has served as the university's provost for a long time. O. Arthur kept him when he arrived as president since O. Arthur likes to run the academic side as well as all other sides himself and has had no desire for a strong provost. Hesseltine has not had an idea or an academic impulse for many years. A thin, ascetic man with a big smile, he is fond of functions. He loves to chum around with whatever trustees will abide him and is fascinated with big-time business, with entrepreneurship. Lee Iacocca and Sam Walton are his heroes. His ineffectiveness on the academic side has not been a recent problem since O. Arthur has loved to micromanage the academic side as well as everything else in sight. This has left Provost Hesseltine, long out of his professional field of statistics as either researcher or teacher, free to pontificate, to tend to the university's ceremonies and in general busy-bee about.

"On the positive side, I have named a new dean for the College of Humanities and Sciences, to replace Jack Bompers. This person will be on board next month," O. Arthur says, breaking into Stanley's thoughts.

"Oh? I hadn't heard. Who is he?"

"She."

"Oh— Well, good for you, Mr. President."

"Yes. I have done it. There does not seem to be any great joy in Mudville, except in women's studies quarters, but I have done it. She was the dean at Wampton, you know, a smaller place, granted, a college, but I think she is qualified. Of course, it will take her a while to get tracked. . . . Yes, I think a very smart, pleasant, good person, very feminine, with a mind like the proverbial steel trap. We hope. Dean Burns. Yes. Dr. Alice Pendleton Burns, two books in the field of religious studies. Interdisciplinary stuff—faith and story, ritual and tribal art. So long, Morris."

"Yes, sir," says Stanley. "Thanks so much for coming by. Take care. Do take good care of yourself."

Stanley feels as if he would like to quote from Kipling's "If," but he can't think of any relevant lines.

O. Arthur Biggs waves, going out.

"I was listening, in the kitchen," Olive says. "I think that is perfectly wonderful, about the new woman dean for the College. But, by gosh, that's scary about dear little O. Arthur. But it's irrelevant, Stanley—do you hear me?—it's all really irrelevant right now, to you! I want you to promise me— Promise me, Stanley, and I mean, you had better: Don't you even think for a minute of getting mixed up in it, of taking on any 'new assignment,' now, or anytime this year! You hear?"

Stanley hears. There is nothing he wants to do less than get mixed up in it.

"Relax," he says to her. "I promise."

Olive forbids him to go on campus to get caught up and involved in all the machinations there, but the next day she allows him to mind her shop for a couple of hours while she goes with her sister Rose to the Gift Market. She knows he is getting stir-crazy, needs to get out of the house. She is afraid he may fall off the stool or lock himself in the bathroom or give away the store while she is gone but hopes he will be all right for a short while. She waves to him and goes off with Rose, praying she is not committing an act of folly.

Stanley sits up on the stool behind the counter. He feels pretty strong by now. He has his sea legs and does not tire so easily. It is a pleasant shop full of all kinds of knicks and knacks, this and that, baby blankets and silver rattles and specialty foods and teas and picture frames and throws and mugs with his university's seal on them and such like stuff in the gift field.

A man in a suit comes in and inquires whether Stanley has something for a gift to mollify his wife. He has hurt her feelings by not noticing she has cut her hair short and dyed it red. Stanley murmurs that is probably beyond the shop's reach, perhaps he should go over to Neiman Marcus.

Stanley turns on the radio that Olive and Rose keep in the shop so they can listen to and ridicule the conservative talk show host Peter Doom, or whoever he is, who is a moron but whose idiot callers amuse them. He turns the AM dial to "The Music of Your Life." He listens to the Mills Brothers singing in harmony about wanting to have a paper doll so other fellows cannot steal her, which has always seemed funny to him if not abnormal. He listens to the song in which the fellow says he'll walk alone because to tell the truth he is lonely. Stanley finds the sentiment tautological. He listens to Teresa Brewer belting out a ditty popular when he was in high school having to do with putting another nickel-in-the-nickelodeon, the result being the twin blisses of lovin' and music, music, music. Ah, the richness and complexity of the early music of his life! Stanley feels sorry for all the older middle-class white people in this city sitting lonely by their radios to whom this station panders. He turns the radio off in fear that it will play "Tenderly."

Hearing a noise like the strutting and fretting of hens, Stanley looks up to see what he estimates to be about fifty elderly women in those rayon pantsuits that are seldom worn anymore except by midwestern women on bus tours. They are crowded into and out beyond the doorway of the shop. Actually as he gets a closer count there are about a dozen, some with wigs, some wearing scarves, all it seems with eyeglasses perched on their noses. One with a handbag big enough to lift the shop comes forward to take point and speak to him as the others begin to pick the merchandise to pieces. She fixes him with a piercing eye.

"What do you have that is novel or interesting?" she demands.

"Oh," Stanley says, "not much of anything, I'm afraid."

"Well, we'll see if you do or not!"

She wheels off around the wall and in a second clutches a variety box of spicy hot sauces, hot pickled okra and industrial strength hot chili peppers and powders. She comes back and waves it at him.

"Oh, I can't sell you that," Stanley says. "That would be too hot and spicy for you. Where are you folks from?"

"Indiana," she says. "We'll see about that! Too hot, eh? We can eat anything in Indiana—"

"In Indiana we can eat anything, you mean, for goodness sakes, Gertrude!" cackles the woman next to her, an obvious grammarian.

"Look here, Alma—girls—have you seen this here?" says the first one. "This will spice your husbands up!"

"How many boxes do you have of this?" says another lady, wattles quivering, eyes gleaming.

"I don't know. Looks like enough for one apiece, there. You'll have to count 'em," Stanley says, not moving off his stool. "But I can't take credit cards. I'm just filling in here for my wife, and I can't work the credit card machine."

"You think we don't have cash, do you?" says the first lady. "Well, how much is it? You'll need your cash for this, girls. You can get some more back at the hotel."

It takes Stanley a while to figure out the sales tax, but he manages to do so and sells for cash a box of the hot stuff to each lady in the pack but one, who buys a nice silver picture frame. They all smile and wave and thank him kindly.

"Is it really all that spicy?" the first lady says.

"Supposed to be. No fooling. I myself would not get near it."

"Hah! I bet you can't get the like of this in Indiana!"

"I bet so," says Stanley. "Well, thanks." These are nice, fierce, independent women. "Glad you came in," he says.

"Is there an ice cream store around here?" one woman says.

He directs them to the Baskin-Robbins a block away.

Olive thinks Stanley looks awfully pleased with himself sitting up on the stool behind the counter when she returns shortly afterwards. He hands her a sheaf of several hundred dollars in small and medium bills. He is so pleased with himself he is insufferable.

She smiles as he tells her and Rose the story. She is glad that this adventure has made him happy.

The next day is D-Day.

Stanley dutifully retraces his steps to the office in the medical building of Doctors Miller, Martz and Wu.

"Hi, I'm Jeff Martz," young Dr. Martz says, coming in. He is a pleasant and professional young fellow, sandy-haired and handsome.

"I remember you," Stanley says, shaking hands. "I looked up and saw you and Dr. Miller when I was going under. It was Rosh Hashanah. I said a prayer to you."

"Looks like it was effective. I think we had a good day that day. How long has it been now?"

"Oh, a month. A month and four days."

"Good. That's about right. Let's take a look here. Any problems?"

"No—"

"Good. Nurse— You know Amanda? Sure. Lie down here. That's right, on your back. Good man. OK, Amanda—"

KA-BOOM!

Before Stanley knows what's up Martz has released the catheter. It is a feeling like his penis has exploded, been blown away. It is a moment of the most intense surprise, pain and pressure. Stanley shuts his eyes, praying that he won't die. They make artificial penises, don't they?

He opens his eyes and looks to the white ceiling above. He is sure it will be covered with pieces—shards and bits—of the flesh and blood and veins of his former penis—

"Fine. Looks good," says Dr. Martz. "Well, sir. Good luck."

Stanley feels and looks. His member is intact. Now he feels no particular pain, no strain, just a little itching, burning in the center. He must suppose it will be all right.

"Let him lie there a minute, Amanda." Dr. Martz turns to go, says "Good luck" again. Stanley knows he means it, means just that. He thinks of what Dr. Miller said at the beginning about possible effects. He thinks of the tough time Jack Bompers has had. Then he thinks he's not Jack. He has taken it easy for a month, just as the doctor said. There need be no bad results. If there are, so be it. The evil thing is gone. He can live with the other, with various forms of degradation, if need be. He hopes he can. "Good luck." Yes, young Martz, he means it. This is the beginning of Phase II. Operation Peeing on Your Own. It is terrifying. Part of him wishes he never had to use the dear old thing again for anything, could just retire it, put it out to pasture. He feels the beginning urge that he is going to have to pee. Dear God . . .

He straightens up, reaching for his pants.

"Here's your diaper," the nurse, Amanda, says. "You had better wear it home."

"Thank you," Stanley says. Awkwardly he puts the diaper on, pulls his pants up around it.

Olive has driven him here. He staggers out to her. He feels he needs to go but does not stop at the restroom in the hallway. He rides homeward in the car with only one thought. It's swelling in him now, but he doesn't know if he has the courage to face the test.

He goes slowly upstairs into his own bathroom, faces the commode.

OK.

Shazam.

Well. Dear God.

It's OK.

Yes.

Oh yes.

Oh dear Lord, and Drs. Miller and Martz, and Wu, it is all right. It's fine.

He pees a strong stream and does not dribble at the end.

He sits in his old chair in the den and pulls out a leather copy of Emerson's essays and reads a little bit from "Self-Reliance," then one of his favorite bits from "Compensation."

He sits in the chair for a long time drinking tea until he has to go again. This time he goes downstairs. It's OK. It's fine.

A week later Jack Bompers calls again.

"I am get-ting better, Stan-ley," he says. "I can make it through the day. Did you fi-nally get your cath-e-ter out?"

"Yes. A week ago, Jack. I'm doing fine."

"Oh, that's good. Celeste, Stan-ley has his cath-e-ter out— Stan-ley, are you doing your pe-nile ex-er-cises?"

"No. No, Jack. I don't seem to need to do any—any exercises."

"Oh? Really? Celeste," Jack calls to his wife, "Stan-ley Mor-ris does not have to do an-y pe-nile ex-er-cises—"

CHAPTER
12

STANLEY IS UP AT the crack of dawn. Olive still asleep, he goes downstairs and makes a pot of coffee and pours a cup and looks out to the early-morn gloaming of his ash-treed backyard. It makes him think of Bert and Flo's place at Calm Harbor, looking out to the waterway. That makes him think of the Colonel and his terrible old jokes. What were some of them?

"Well," the Colonel says, "this traveling salesman stops at a farmer's to spend the night, and he eats dinner with the farmer and his wife. There's one piece of pie left for dessert, and they all want it but they leave it on the table and go to bed. There's only one bed, so the salesman gets in it with the farmer and his wife. She cozies up to him, and the farmer goes to sleep. 'Now's your chance,' she says, and the salesman jumps out of bed and goes and eats the pie!"

"I had forgotten," Stanley says.

The Colonel reminds him of the one about the slicker of a salesman who asks directions of an old farmer. The farmer gives him confusing directions. "You're not far from a fool, are you?" says the slicker. "No," says the farmer, "there's just a fence post between us."

"Now I remember," Stanley says, "all your stories tend to be along the same lines."

"That's why I like them," says the Colonel. "Have you heard the one about the traveling salesman who—"

"Enough," says Flo. "You don't have to tell them all at once."

"Isn't she wonderful?" beams the Colonel.

Oh my, Stanley thinks, and stops thinking back. It is a new dawn, a new day for Stanley. He is going to don his tweed jacket and rep tie and go back up to the campus that he loves.

For a moment he sits and thinks about his campus, his university, his place.

It is not great, but it is pretty good. It has been a place that cherishes students, a campus with a conscience. The faculty teach, and some do some pretty good research. Some roam the world or are known around it. It is private, about a third the size of any public university, but involved. Somewhat involved. Stanley sips his coffee and laughs, remembering when he first learned that his dear Highland U. was of but only somewhat in the world, thirty years ago or more when he went up to a conference on Martha's Vineyard with old Dean Doggett. They had gone under the illusion that since Highland was on the edge of a major city it was an "urban" university. They were quickly disabused, and were about the only whites. "You got any idea what a non-middle-class university would even *look like?*" one fellow screamed at the poor old dean.

The next morning Stanley and Dean Doggett sat on the porch of the inn looking to the water, feeling strange and uneasy in the warm sun following the rain of the day before. But one of the black guys from a real urban place came by on a bicycle and waved. "It's nice to be up here with Martha on her vine-yard," he calls to them.

"Say," the gentle old dean says to Stanley, "let's go fishing." And they do, and come back home, and Highland U. has not changed much since.

Stanley hears Olive coming down and rouses from his reverie. He is very eager and a little scared to go back. Stanley knows it is a new day, and not just for him.

It is a bright, crisp October day when Stanley walks back onto the campus. The falling leaves of oaks and elms and maples are brilliantly and blindingly red and orange and yellow. The sunlight on his buildings makes the stones and old brick mellow. The sunlight on the buildings is more mellow, Stanley thinks, than even on the buildings of Oxford. Down at the end of the long main walk the spire of the chapel winks. From the gold-domed science building come the notes of the chimes announcing the hour. Stanley stops on the path to hear each note. Yes: ten o'clock. Quite right.

Look at all the students. Most are still in long droopy shorts though it is fall. More seem to have gone to plain droopy T-shirts instead of those with names and slogans or concert venues on them. More seem to have gone to wearing their ubiquitous gimme caps turned around so the bill points back. They nod and smile and some speak to him and Stanley feels expanded, as if he is having a veritable transfusion of Youth. At the fountain in front of the main building he runs into the tall figure of the chaplain.

The chaplain's demeanor is serious, as he gestures back towards the flagpole where the flag is at half-mast.

"Who has died?" he says to Stanley.

Stanley nods and gestures that he does not know. He is fairly sure it is not himself. With a pained look on his handsome face the chaplain gestures towards the administration building.

"Surely not," Stanley says.

"He has been in and out of the hospital," the chaplain says. "Well—let us keep the faith."

Going into the lobby of his building Stanley meets Grover Hartlington, a noted historian of the Middle Ages. Usually they merely nod but Professor Hartlington seems, with ceremony—as he adjusts his Phi Beta Kappa key on its chain over his belly, smooths his white mane of hair, brushes imaginary flecks from his sleeve, adjusts his steel spectacles—to wish to speak to him. He gestures for Stanley to come closer, then speaks softly into his ear.

"My PSA is three-point-five," he says.

"Well, that's probably OK, if you keep track of it," says Stanley.

"Meyers's is up five points," Hartlington says, mentioning another historian. "Do you know Spence, in Geology, only fifty-five? PSA of seven-something. And Witkowski, the biologist, is having a biopsy this week—he's shot to twelve. I fear it's curtains for Witkowski. So, what is your PSA, I mean, after all—"

He takes off his specs, rubs them with his red bandanna, peers at Stanley as if he were a medieval artifact.

"Zero," Stanley says. "Zero, zero, zero," he doth sing.

"You're damn lucky," hisses the chronicler of the Black Death in his ear.

"Yes," says Stanley, passing on. All things being equal, and the chestnut gone, he is lucky.

He wonders if his fate now is to be kind of a secretary, a keeper of the record, of the male faculty's PSAs: the Brotherhood of the Prostate. It is the one true brotherhood, all right.

He goes up to his office in the southeast corner of the second floor and puts the key in and opens the door and beholds the stacks of books and papers on chairs and desk, the little Oriental rug Olive found years ago, and all the shelves of lovely books.

"Aha," croons his friend and colleague next door from within his sanctum, Hopewell Mirk, a younger, brilliant fellow who truly cares for students and for teaching, "aha-ha-la-la-la—um um yes— Stanley's back, oh how nice, yes—um-la . . . Welcome back— Yes— Oh my word. Stanley, dear Stanley, come home to us now. Oh— yes— How are you? Looking fine— Yes— Good. Good, good. Yes—"

Stanley enters his office to this lullaby of welcome.

At lunchtime he goes to the Faculty Club to join his colleagues on the executive committee of the Faculty Senate. Before going up-stairs, he stops at the table in the corner to greet those there. They are much the same as always, and, he remembers with a pang, as when he brought his brother Mack here for lunch.

"How is your friend, that Mack?" asks Beltrán-Luna, remem-bering too. "He was a noble guy."

Stanley doesn't have it in him to tell him Mack is gone. "Oh, he's fine," he says. "Sort of in limbo right now, but fine."

"Yes," says Professor Beltrán-Luna, the DNA man. "Please tell him when you see him I said hello, and that I also said we must not yield to Tyranny! *Hasta la victoria siempre!*"

"I will tell him," Stanley says.

Upstairs around the dining table in the study are Bobby Lee, the geologist, hat on head; Inder Singh; the pessimist from Stanley's own department, Morrison J. Harrison; Martha Levy, from the B-School; Ken Osmatzoo of Engineering; and the enormously rotund former Rhodes Scholar, red of face and sly of eye, Al McSorly, of Law.

"Welcome back," Morrison Harrison says. "O. Arthur Biggs is dying."

"You have no proof of that," says Inder Singh. "There is no truth in what you humanists say or write, it is all opinion. I think that he, Arthur Biggs, the president, is fine. It clearly is a ruse. It is a trick to lull us into feeling sorry for him while he is forcing upon us this dreadful reengineering which is ruining the university—"

"I don't think O. Arthur is very hot for the reengineering program himself," offers Bobby Lee. "I think that is something coming from the trustees, like the corporations have all been doing."

"How do you know?"

"He told me so."

"Well—" says Inder.

"If you even damn suggest I am a toady to the president," Bobby says, pulling his hat down over his eyes and staring at Inder, "I will take you out to my dig and bury you so deep they will not find you for five hundred years and will wonder when they do what kind of human species we had back now."

Singh smiles, pleased at this show of force if not at the prospect of interment. Stanley thinks of O. Arthur's message to him that because of his heart problems he may have to step aside.

"So, how are we paying for all this reengineering?" inquires Professor Levy, of Organizational Behavior/Business Management.

"From 'funds-functioning-as-endowment,'" Bobby Lee replies.

"What is that?"

"That is the, well, the backup pool of funds, the deep aquifer of the life of the university, now being depleted—depleted—depleted," intones Morrison J. Harrison, head in hands.

Stanley laughs, to himself, he thinks.

"Ah, you think this is humorous, the ruination of the university?" Singh says. "I am not surprised you have come out of hospital with less sense than when you went in, which is little. Is the new dean—what is her name?—to come to us today? Ah God, she is such a woman!"

"Said she'd try," Bobby says. "Wasn't sure. Just on the job, you know."

"By which I mean a *beautiful* woman," says Inder. "Ah, I would be toady to such a dean!"

"Oh my," says Martha Levy. "My, my, my."

"What do you mean?"

"Cross-cultural ironic reverse sexism, your remark, wasn't it?"

"Ah, yes! Of course. I am glad you understand, I am speaking like a man, like a Sikh."

"Well," says Martha, of OBBM, "I'd reorganize the joint for them for a lot less—just a hundred thousand or so. What are they calling it, the reengineering project?"

"Project Daedalus," says Stanley, smiling. He has read, or tried to, a recent description of this "reengineering" project.

"Oh," intones Morrison J. Harrison, "let us fly ever closer to the sun . . ."

"'Tis the labyrinth for us," McSorly says.

"OK," says Bobby Lee, "what you got on the bloody University Calendar, Ken?"

"The students," advises Professor Osmatzoo, "are proposing a fourteen-week term with a four-day Fall Break in October."

"Jesus Christ. Again?"

"This will not work, because of labs in science courses. Of course, for humanists, for whom all is totally in the realm of opinion, and research and verification are unnecessary, truth a shimmer of subjectivity, the length of term does not matter. For humanists, as we all know, a three-week semester is sufficient. Often they teach such 'short courses,' calling them, shamefully, 'mini-terms,' to say nothing of the short little courses for full semester credit often taught in such vocational and nonintellectual new disciplines as painting, music, photography, the throwing of pots—ceramics— which have no place in the curriculum of a legitimate university at all but thrive in ours—"

"Music is a new discipline? Oh, your ignorance, my man," Mc-Sorly says.

Leaving them to this discussion, Stanley goes down the hall to relieve himself. All remains well, sure and strong, controlled. As he finishes, a sharp rap comes on the door.

"Excuse me," he calls, looking to see he has not locked the door, zipping and flushing. "Just a minute, here."

Hearing no answer he washes and dries his hands before opening the door to the hallway, expecting the intruder to have fled. But as, somewhat flustered, he opens the door, he sees a female person standing there.

"Is this for men, or women, or both, or what?" she says, looking at him intently, holding onto the strap of a large purse set in military fashion over her shoulder.

"Men. I mean, it is not marked, but I have always assumed— that it is for men."

"Ah!" she says, rolling her dark eyes at him and at whatever audience she must imagine is watching this confrontation. "You men!"

Then she smiles at him saucily and gives him a quick poke in the ribs. "Well," she says, "if this isn't it, I suppose you guys put one downstairs, for the ladies, eh?"

"Oh yes— The one downstairs—"

The eyes are chocolate brown. Her hair is dark. She is rather tall. She is assertive but merry as a lark. She seems to grin, not smile, at him.

"You men!" she says again, and marches off down the hall, and dances down the stairs. He returns to the study and sits at the long table and leans to speak to Harrison and McSorly; but they look from him, and suddenly rise, the massive McSorly heaving his girth upright and smiling an Irish smile and semibowing while the face of the pessimistic, often bitter Dickens and Hardy scholar Morrison J. Harrison is transformed into a young boy's face, a look that would have graced the face of that "good man" Mr. Pickwick, as Bobby Lee rises, removes his old desert hat with a flourish and announces, as in she skips, bathroom found and mission accomplished, grinning, eyes on each of them in turn like dark magnets, "Gentlemen—Martha—our dean. Dean Burns, let me present to you the Ex Comm—"

Stanley stands to greet her, also. She goes around the table, shaking each hand. Each introduces him- or herself to her. Dean Burns acknowledges each. To Stanley she says, "President Biggs told me about you. You've been here a long time, haven't you? He said you were part of the fundament."

Stanley nods, a bit embarrassed but not too much. Firmament, pediment, fundament, what the hell.

"He has been forever," Professor Singh says, looking at her appraisingly, obviously delighted by what he sees. "He is irrationally loyal. He has been a toady to all the deans we have had, a ridiculous succession of them, in the College. Undoubtedly, he will be a toady to you as well."

"Golly, I sure hope so," says Dean Alice Pendleton Burns, Godiva eyes lit up, not grinning now but smiling at Stanley warmly.

They sit around the table and talk of many things. Bobby Lee says the faculty may be willing to consider a gentle form of post-tenure review if it is encouraging and does not lead to dismissals.

"Sure!" whoops Alice P. Burns. She seems high energy, a bright spirit.

They talk about this reengineering phenomenon, corporate business models being thrust upon the university.

"Of course, a little efficiency wouldn't hurt," says Martha Levy.

"I really love that old glass sign on the stand at the cashier's window that says 'Wait Here For Next Available Clerk.' It looks like the nineteen-twenties. What's the computer literacy situation here?" the new dean asks.

"The students seem to know how to use them," says Morrison J. Harrison, sneering.

"How about you?"

He looks at her as from a great distance. "I write on Hardy," he says. "One cannot write on Hardy on a word processor."

Hardy har har, Stanley thinks. He looks at the dean. She seems also to be suppressing mirth. He gets the strange feeling she may even be experiencing the same mental blip.

Telling them she will be counting on the support of them all, she rises and bounces around the table and shakes the hand of each of them. She gives Stanley a quick firm one.

"You walking back?" she says. They are in the same building.

"You bet," says Stanley.

Trying to keep up with her as she lopes along down the path, Stanley says, "Were you an athlete in college?"

She reminds him of a blind date he had as a freshman who was a bit taller than he was and who had come down out of the Green Mountains of Vermont.

"Sure," she says.

"Track, I'll bet. Or volleyball?"

She shakes her head. "Basketball," she says. "USC. All PAC-Ten."

At home he says to Olive, "I met the new dean at the meeting. She is something."

"By which you mean?"

"Oh, I don't know. Different. Jack Bompers she ain't."

"Well, of course not. I bet you guys have a long way to go getting used to a woman dean! Now, Stanley, I want you to be nice to her and to try to help her in that maze of prejudice and privilege and random goodwill and guilt you call a university. Don't let her get hit from the blind side or fall in a hole. You know? Let's have her over, her and her husband, whom she doubtless calls her 'spouse.' What does he do? Husbands of deans have to do quite a bit or not much of anything, usually quite a bit. Anyway, you know so much about the place, that's a good role for you now, to be kind of her old uncle, Uncle Stanley, avuncular Professor Morris, the statesman, advisor, behind the arras. Right?"

"The pompous fool, you mean?" Stanley laughs. "Hell, yes. I can do that."

CHAPTER
13

THINKING OF MACK, STANLEY calls Milton Hooser, Mack's former partner with whom he has stripped Mack's apartment of its sheets and mattresses and who since has assisted him with Mack's affairs. Stanley has been executor for Mack's estate. He has not had much to do.

"Can we wind this up now?" he says to Milton.

"There is a bit of stock that's left to be transferred to the kids, that's about it," says Milton. "Oh—except for that half acre he bought over by the lake. You know? Bought it two-three years ago, through one of those promo deals. Bought it for ninety-nine dollars, I think. I remember he went over there and came back laughing because of course it wasn't even on or by the lake. He bought it, though. Why would he do that? Just an impulse, I guess."

"No," Stanley says. "I don't think so. Mack didn't do many impulsive things, even for just ninety-nine bucks. He knew he was getting conned, but he kept paying taxes on it. I paid the tax on it already for this year."

"Beats me," says Milton Hooser. "Anyway, I guess you could sell it back to the developers. Or pass it on to the kids, though I doubt they'd want the little piece of nothing. We do need to keep it or let it go, before the final filing."

"OK," Stanley says. "Thank you, Milton. I'm glad you are doing well."

"Yeah. I'm doing fine. With a good firm. I miss him, though, you know. He was a great teacher . . ."

"Yes," says Stanley.

Cove Hills is about eighty miles away. On Sunday Stanley asks Olive to drive him there. It takes about two hours by the time they find where the little plot must be by the developer's plat map from which Mack bought it. Anyway, no one could find it exactly since the half acre is somewhere in the midst of a hilled forest a mile or more from Lake Boone. This is hillier country than the city and its environs where Stanley and Olive live. The trees are more like those of Stanley's boyhood home. Stanley leaves Olive sitting in the car, with the windows up and doors locked, on the asphalt road and walks into the wooded hillside. Leaves carpet the ground under the tall trees, and needles from the pines. They had no pines there then, when Stanley was growing up, but yes, this is like—anyway, at least *like*— the woods they roamed as boys after picking the berries and watering the hills of spuds and the tomato plants and feeding the chickens and milking the goats on their fathers' places in the home country.

Yes. That was why Mack had laughed at the con men but had gone ahead and bought it, insisting they give him the come-on price and exactly that God's little half acre advertised: it reminded him of home, of being Shawnee or Iroquois along the trails of the then deep woods of home.

So—what does it mean? That he must keep it, hold on to this psychic place, even now, for Mack? Yes, Stanley thinks, standing in the warm dappled enclosure of trunks and twisted branches and leaves on trees and on the ground, I guess that's what's being told me . . .

"No, old buddy, my brother, Stan the Man," Mack says. "It's OK. Sell it. I don't need it now. I'm getting free, and freer all the time. The kids don't want or need or understand it. Who could understand it, Stanley, but you and me? I would come here and stand in here every once in a while, and it would make me happy or it would make me sad. Hell, I was so screwed up I hardly knew. But sell it. Get rid of it. You still need your garden, I know, Stanley, and your house, and what?—all the symbols that speak to you. But I'm OK now. I really am. I can almost understand and forgive myself, by now. I really can."

"How is your buddy—your other buddy—?"

Stanley could not say the name, not wishing to be presumptuous.

"OK. Fine. Put me on my own, now. So—"

Now they are walking out of the woods together, on the strip of asphalt road, towards Stanley's big old car. Mack laughs.

"What?" says Stanley.

"Why, it's like pledgeship, Stan. I'm up for initiation now, you know? It's like—oh, crossing over. You know—"

"Sure," Stanley says. "That's what I thought. Mom—Flo—told me— She used to talk to people, oh, my grandmothers, others close to her, who would come to her when they were 'crossing over.' I'm glad you don't need to run. Just to run and run—now—Mack—"

Stanley hears the click of the car door unlocking, the whisper of the window rolling down.

"I believe you talk to yourself more than you did before the operation," Olive says.

"Not really," he says, going around and getting in the other side. "I was talking to Mack, you see."

"Oh," she says. "I see."

Stanley looks at her. She isn't just saying so. She does see. She understands. They clasp hands lightly before she shifts into drive and turns the steering wheel.

"What did Mack say to do with it?" she says.

"We are going to sell it. It reminded him of growing up, but he said go ahead and let it go, now."

"Moving on, eh?" Olive says.

"Sure," says Stanley. "Moving on."

They return home to a call from Morrison Harrison telling them that O. Arthur Biggs has taken a leave of absence because of the condition of his heart and that Provost T. Herbert Hesseltine has been named acting president by the board of trustees.

CHAPTER
14

THE AMIABLE ACTING PRESIDENT, Herb Hesseltine, who often parks on the wrong side of grammar, syntax, and metaphor, presides at a general faculty meeting and gives them a Pep Talk. He hopes they will all get on the reengineering bandwagon, mount Daedalus and ride it up into the sky. "What I am hopeful," he says, "is that we can all get behind the wheel and get some steam in our sails here and set sail for better productivity and a better bottom line as a university."

Inder Singh rises to inquire where the faculty might fit in such a ship. Is this not a matter of more efficient administrative and student services?

"Yes," says Hesseltine. He is a reed of a man with eyes dimmed by peering and poring through sheets of statistics first as an accountant, then an accounting professor, and for some years now an administrator. "But we all do these things together and the faculty have got to help keep their eye on the ball, on the consumer. The consumer better be happy, or the university is in big trouble. And we have some unhappy customers out there—students who wonder what is the relevance of what they study, parents who wonder why in the world they have got to pay so much, and trustees, those type consumers."

Martha Levy stands and says, "The university is not a business. If I wanted to be in business, I would be in business, and making a lot more, too. You know what I mean, Herb?"

"Certainly, my dear," Hesseltine says, "but we must all now ask the big question together— What is our product? Who are our consumers? Like, Taco Bell in their reengineering effort did not just ask, 'Who eats junk food?' Taco Bell asked the big question! Taco Bell asked, 'Who eats food?'"

"Ah—um—la de la— Yes," hums Hopewell Mirk, sitting next to Stanley in the auditorium. "Um—um—um— Yes, yes. Of course, the Big Burrito. Um, ha— 'Who eats food?' Ah, indeed. The Larger Question. Um—la de da . . ."

"Soon we will have a daylong staff and faculty meeting to explore and elucidate these crucial matters," Herb Hesseltine promises, and opens the floor to the faculty.

Stanley is too perturbed to participate in the discussion.

He goes to have his checkup for the PSA and then to visit O. Arthur Biggs in his room in the hospital just a floor up from where he himself sojourned after his operation.

In the offices of Miller, Martz and Wu, he is greeted by young Dr. Martz, who informs him that Dr. Miller, his hero, has packed up and left and gone to Idaho to practice, a small managed care practice, and mainly to hunt and fish. Dr. Miller just got fed up with all the red tape of big-time practice and all the tax and legal and professional crapola, Martz tells Stanley.

"But his hands," says Stanley, "those incredible hands . . ."

"He sure does have the hands," says Martz. "My God, wonderful hands, small as a child's hands, precious instruments, those hands." He looks at his own quite capable hands. "So I'm your doctor now."

"Fine," says Stanley. "I can't believe that he would just up and go, just leave."

"He was coiled up like a spring," says Dr. Martz. "He had moved way up north to Allen and gotten himself a Range Rover just to drive in the city. I think he would have exploded if he hadn't gotten out of here. Didn't Hemingway end up in Idaho, Professor?"

"Yes," says Stanley, "but it didn't bring him peace of mind."

Martz chuckles, as if that is a good one. Stanley's PSA remains at zero zero zero. That really *is* a good one.

On the way to see O. Arthur, Stanley stops in to visit Norwick Baine, a physics professor, a man several years older than himself. The chaplain has told him that Baine is in the hospital recuperating from a prostatectomy. He is not doing well. They did not get it all and he is having urinary complications. Norwick looks shrunken and frightened lying on the hospital bed, Mrs. Baine trying to be upbeat hovering over him. His white-haired head looks shriveled, as if headhunters had shrunk it. Stanley feels guilty telling Norwick he himself is doing well. But the old physicist smiles at him sweetly. As often the best scientists are, he is a true humanist who reads widely and once confessed to Stanley that he writes poetry. In the hallway outside Norwick's room Stanley murmurs to Ruth Baine that things might get better, with the radiation, and so on . . .

"No," she says, a spare, gray-eyed lady. "He is a realist. He knows exactly his condition. I know he appreciates your visit, Dr. Morris. And President Hesseltine came by. I thought that was awfully nice."

Yes, Stanley nods. It was.

He goes into Art Biggs's room shaking his head. "What's with you?" he says. "You're in and out of here like a yo-yo. This isn't like you, Arthur."

"I'm fine," O Arthur Biggs barks. "I keep having flare-ups. They keep giving me tests. I can't seem to eat much. Who could eat? How's Hesseltine? Seems he should be fairly harmless for a brief interim. Eh? Hell, I should be back by early spring. But I hear the fellow has the faculty all upset already?"

Stanley sits and smiles and tells O. Arthur about Taco Bell.

O. Arthur Biggs snorts. "The state our university is in, with enrollment edging down, Morris, Herb is right. We do have to ask those questions, get a little efficiency in the system, get you guys teaching more— Eh? With the state of things maybe we should ask the question, 'Who eats hospital food?' Ha. How is Dean Burns? She done anything yet? You guys forgiving her for being a woman?"

"Lovely. I mean, I think she's holding her own—doing fine."

"Lovely? My ass, Stanley. What's she *doing?*"

"Well, for one thing, she seems to be circling me like a lion about to pounce. I'm afraid she's going to ask me to do something."

"Of course she is. I told her to. The damn Task Force on Human and Academic Values. We need it, Stanley, in the larger context. The world, our society, our city, our curriculum, our very relevance. Where the Top Line meets the Bottom Line. You dig?"

"Herb told the Ex Comm that he saw no need for such a task force, that we would be fine if we just each taught our courses and left the larger picture, which I take it in his mind is an administrative matter, to him."

Stanley thinks O. Arthur is going to reach into his deeper bag of expletives. But he does not. Very seriously he says, "So talk to him on his own terms, Stanley. Tell him if we're going to ask, 'Who eats food?' we also really do have to ask, 'What is its nutritional value?' You know?"

Stanley nods. Of course he knows. Then he looks out the window at the panorama of cars and buildings he remembers seeing from his own hospital room in this building and does not answer directly. He cannot commit to taking on a task for Dean Alice Burns. He has promised Olive. She has told him to help the new woman dean but to do it in the side lane. He wants nothing to do with Herb Hesseltine, who he is sure is doing his best in his unexpected situation. Stanley just wants, now, to continue healing, to be Stanley, to teach, to—what? (To sit here with his ailing friend and leader and think like Hamlet? "Jesus, Stanley," some voice within him says.) Ah, that this solid flesh would get a little bit more solid, eh, isn't that the question, and the answer? Stanley thinks it is, in this moment. And acknowledges in his heart that, unlike this courageous guy lying so fitfully in the bed in this room, maybe he himself, Stanley Morris, is no better than Inder Singh or Morrison Harrison or the rest of them who, if the truth were known, relish sitting in their safe and tenured place and speaking up and out as long as it's safe and no one can really challenge or get back at them. Well.

"Maybe," he says to Art, looking at him again. Art's good eye is closed and his dead one is staring off across the room sideways.

"Maybe I could talk to Herb, try to be kind of an advisor to him. Not that I know a damn thing about all this stuff that he—that we—are into. But you and I came to have a pretty good relationship, as prof and president."

O. Arthur pops open the trenchant eye and smiles at him and his bad eye drifts over to be in sync with the good one.

"Yes, we do," he says. "But—" He shakes his head.

O. Arthur Biggs is tired. He reaches and picks up a book. Stanley gives him a little wave and leaves.

On Wednesday his graduate student Joe Green comes by, looking sheepish.

"I'm leaving, Professor Morris," he says. "Packing it up. My dissertation is terrible. It's just lying there with all them stupid note cards and frozen up as a dead dog. I've been avoiding having a conference with you. All I've been doing lately is taking all the note cards and putting them into the computer. Some creative effort, huh? Oh boy, I'm sorry. But I'm really not. I need to go, get out of here, at least for a while."

They walk from the front yard around the house and into the back yard. Joe has been trimming and mowing for him, and it's in good shape. There are a lot of leaves on the ground, but Stanley thinks maybe he is up to raking and sacking them. You have to put them in big biodegradable paper sacks which the city sells you if you want them hauled away, these days. He should of course make a mulch pile, fix a bin or whatever the hell you do, to accommodate all the leaves back out here, use 'em on the garden in the summer. Add the coffee grounds and eggshells and stir lightly.

"It could go right here, I guess," Stanley says.

"Sir?"

"The mulch pile, Joe. Whatever you call it. Right here behind the barn. I mean, the garage."

"This is where the garden goes, Professor Morris. We're going to get a rotor-tiller and double the size of it. Do corn and squash. Or— you are. Aren't you? You're going to go ahead and plant it in the spring, aren't you?"

"Don't know, Joe. I'll wait and see. I mean, I guess I am. Maybe you'll come back by then, get tired of New Orleans and the music scene. I hope that you will come back."

"Oh. Well. Maybe. I mean, maybe I'll even go back home and go to Ag school. Who knows? I may turn out to be not much more of a jazz player in my older age than I am a scholar."

Joe laughs. Stanley realizes how uncertain Joe is.

"Shouldn't you stay here until the end of this semester? It's just a month and a half, Joe. It would be wise, you see, to get the credit in the courses you are taking . . ."

"No. Got to go. Got to move it. Harry says there's right now a place for me in a group there. So who knows, Professor Morris, who knows? I've blown off my courses pretty good, so I suppose it's what you call—what? A moot point. Just academic?"

"I guess that's what you call it. 'Academic.' Oh hell, Joe, I'm sorry I made you teach those two courses of mine—though I appreciate your doing it more than I can say. I know it made you get behind in your own teaching and in progress on the dissertation—"

"Listen, sir. You've said that. I know you do. It was great. I love the students. It was a humongous favor that you did me. Gee whiz, I told you, I'm a terrible teacher. I can't quite get it right. I can get in the rhythm, get in the flow, in music but not quite get there in the teaching. It's so weird. You don't realize because it's your nature, and you just know a lot and you're there and into it, and it's cool, you just do it. I mean, like, I bet you enjoy teaching *grammar*, even. Right?"

Yes, Stanley thinks, grammar holds the forms of thought together. Nods, yes, to Joe.

"Yeah. Say, look here, these bees are still hanging in here, in October. Just swirling around real slow. What have you decided to do about 'em? You going to get rid of them or leave 'em be?"

"Don't know, Joe. Don't know." Stanley has forgotten about the bees that seem to stay forever around his house, his garage, his yard. Olive has not mentioned them. He supposes she thinks they're gone.

A couple of them come and loop lazily around his head as he stands a little closer to the back of the old garage. They do not buzz. They have always been quiet bees. "Kill 'em," he says, but not aloud, not to Joe, not even really to himself, for he does not mean it. He is never going to kill the bees or do anything mean or stupid to get rid of them. He poisoned them once but would not do so again.

He is just so very sad and sorry that Joe is leaving. Except for Olive, it has been a long time since he has come to depend on anyone as he has done with Joe Green, whose many and varied talents may yet bring him back this way again or take him away on roads neither he nor Joe imagines now.

In the called meeting of faculty and staff Herb Hesseltine has brought in a real pitchman of a reengineering expert, Pete Pointer by name. He is out of Houston—Stanley thinks maybe the fellow has done an earlier turn as a televangelist there—and out of sight. That is, he is a hardheaded, pragmatic, businesslike, and practical man with a mystical vein, and dwells in a world of soft metaphor. Like any salesman, he opens up with a few jokes to get their attention.

"People don't like to hear about reengineering," he then confides. "They are hostile to it."

"Um. Ah," says Hopewell Mirk, half dozing in his seat. "How true, how true. Tereu."

"Reengineering consultants are *hated*," Pete Pointer says.

"Imagine that," says Hopewell, beside Stanley.

"Hated by those who *resist change!* Are you among them?"

"Um. Yes. La, la. Indeed." Hopewell dutifully raises his hand to be counted among the elect. Inder and Harrison and McSorly join him in the gesture.

"But you will perish if you think this is all just a bunch of sound and fury not signifying anything. This is *hard*. This is tactical, pragmatic. This is a form of *battle*. This is *change*. 'May you live in interesting times,' says the old Chinese—"

"Cliché," says Hopewell.

"Look at the larger context! Look all around you! Has there ever been a time of greater change than this world we live in?"

Several historians and anthropologists in the audience nod, offering examples of times of similar dynamic change and restructuring in the known world. A weathered geologist offers dinosaurs.

"We must not be guilty of the arrogance of resisting change. I sense resistance in you, here, among the *faculty!* Your staff look fairly cool, fairly with it, to me, but you faculty—! We must all come together with the two key qualities—*humility*—and *striving*—"

"Ah, yes. Um. The humble Dr. Faustus, always forging ahead—um de la—with his light under his little bushel—so proud, so humble . . . Yes . . ."

"Hopewell," says Stanley, "give the guy a chance."

"Why? Ah? Scotch him," Hopewell says. "Dangerous. A crazy fellow."

"It is an inexorable, an ineluctable logic!" Pointer pants. "It is an unopposable force. It rains on the just and the unjust! Only change is security. This force I bring comes along with total objectivity like the force of historical necessity—"

"Oh my," says Morrison.

"Where is Vaclav when you need him?" asks McSorly.

"—and it picks the low-hanging fruit. Then it picks the higher fruit. It is a key combo of desperation—distribution—foresight—alternative thinking— It is a new map for the territory—"

"Could it be a 'Right Name'?" says Harrison Morrison or whatever the hell his name is. "'Language in Thought and Action'?"

"—and in your case, you faculty, the low-hanging fruit is—*tenure!* Everything that even *looks like tenure* is under attack, my friends—ha-ha ha—in the rest of the world!"

"The object of tenure," retorts Bobby Lee, who has studied civilizations of East and West around the world, with his old hat on his head, "is to protect the obligation of the scholar-teacher to challenge what is spurious, in the faith that the fallacious is revealed and truth confirmed by a free give and take of ideas."

"I give up," Pete Pointer says. "I have never encountered such obduracy. Why, when I lecture at major corporations, they do not challenge what I say—"

Herb Hesseltine jumps up, looking very pinstriped and severe.

"Gosh durn, Pete," he says, when he gets the audience's attention, and the consultant has skulked into the corner already packing his charts and graphs and the key-concepts video he was going to show, "I'm sorry. We have obviously got a long way to go here. I apologize."

Some staff and a few faculty applaud. The chaplain goes down to shake Herb's hand. This seems pretty courageous to Stanley.

"Well," he says to Hopewell and Harrison, as they stand together without much wind in their sails. Feeling a punch on his shoulder, he turns to see Dean Burns, a frown on her face, peering at him.

"So you think there's not a huge need for thinking through human and academic values around here?" she demands.

On the way back to his building Stanley meets his former student Q-Man along the campus path. Q-Man seems even stockier and stronger, he seems to have put on weight and to have even more muscles than when he was going up the mountain in the summer.

"How are you, man?" he says.

"I am doing well, all things considered."

"Excellent! That's golden, man! Oh, I knew you would be! Quality, Professor— Quality!"

In his office Stanley finds an e-mail message from his brother Barry up at his college in New Jersey. Barry had proclaimed that it was like the coming together of the Union Pacific and the Southern Pacific at Promontory Point, Utah, that is to say, historic, when the Morris brothers—two technological dunces—first exchanged e-mail.

Stump seasoning nicely, Stanley reads on the screen from bmorris@post.cis.cju.edu. *Have new Foot. Back on Faculty Senate.*

New President here a moron. Will thrash him with my Foot in hand. Fits well also in mouth. Have three course preparations. Get to work, Stanley.

OK, Stanley replies mentally to his brother Barry.

In his mind he sees Barry, lip curling, planted on prosthetic foot, at full height, excoriating the new president for whatever folly to the faculty . . .

And thanks his brother for the message.

CHAPTER
15

"You are one of the ones I'm coming by to see—because I know you really loved the man."

"I beg your pardon?" Stanley says. As he was when Milton Hooser appeared in his office to bring him the news of Mack's suicide, Stanley has been reading student papers. He has been getting some good essays and stories now from his classes. He is pleased at how well his teaching is going.

"President Biggs. O. Arthur. Died this morning. Early. Back at home. Passed away in his sleep. Very peacefully, I understand."

"Oh. Why— Oh shit, Andy. I would have thought he'd rage—rage like hell—"

"The Lord came and took him peacefully."

"Oh, prune juice, Chaplain."

"I beg your pardon?"

Stanley puts down his red marking pen. He massages his marking hand with the other. He looks around the office. On his top shelf is a little lacquered stuffed bullfrog playing a stand-up bass fiddle. He wishes he had shown it to Art Biggs. O. Arthur would have liked that. He doesn't feel very religious right now, with earnest Andy leaning toward him like he is needing industrial strength spiritual help. It is not fair, he thinks. It isn't very damn fair at all—to O. Arthur, to his wife, to the university. My God, to the university! It isn't fair to Stanley. Why, at bottom he felt all along that O. Arthur Biggs would return, that the bumbler Hesseltine would go back to his statistics sheets and do little harm or even some good, just until the spring.

Sure. Spring will come, all right. O. Arthur Biggs will just not be here to experience it with us. Oh my. Oh hell. Oh goddamn it all to hell.

"I'm fine," he says to the chaplain, before he asks, straightening in his chair, folding his hands together.

"It's all right to cry," Andy says. "I feel your tears. I really do. I—admired—him too. And loved him, of course."

"Of course," says Stanley. "I want to thank you for coming. For telling me. Before I ran into someone in the hall—or saw the flag at half-mast and had to ask who, or read it in the paper."

"I visited with him."

"And you think he had come to terms with it, with his mortality, and dying?"

"Oh no. Not at all. He wasn't acknowledging it. He had no intention of going. I think he was a lot like you, and others I have witnessed, who keep winking at but have no real belief in it and just treat it as the great Absurdity, the Absurd Joke. I wonder what kind of faith can let people, as they get pretty far along, do that. I wonder if it's faith at all, or just ego, or something else."

"I wonder," Stanley says.

"I think O. Arthur is pretty surprised right now," the chaplain says.

"*Is?*"

"Yes."

"Do you believe in spirits?"

"The spirit. Yes. All is really spirit, isn't it?"

"I mean, like angels."

"Oh, angels." The chaplain beams, as if this is a good one indeed. Pop culture belief. Angels.

"I believe our earthly body assumes the form of spirit. And I believe in the usual articles of faith, of resurrection and so on."

"Angels," Stanley says, nodding vigorously at him.

"You believe in angels?"

"You bet your big silver cross you wear at Commencement I do," Stanley says. "Yes, sir. You bet your life I do."

The chaplain looks at him quizzically, as if he has a little different problem with Stanley than he thought he had.

It makes Stanley want to laugh. But he doesn't. He doesn't want Andy to think he's totally nuts. But he looks around the office, in all the corners, remembering Mack and Jesus, and halfway thinking he will see O. Arthur Biggs sitting there enjoying the conversation.

And it makes him feel a hell of a lot better about Art. It's a terrible shame, and a blow to all of them, that he had to leave so soon. But Stanley knows he is out there somewhere, starting up the trail.

After they go to O. Arthur's funeral, Stanley and Olive come home and look at each other.

"May I fix you the best dry vodka martini you ever had?" he says.

"Sure," she says, looking a bit startled.

Carefully he fixes it for her and in a short glass with two cubes of ice pours himself a generous measure of The Famous Grouse, that which Bobby Lee brought to him as a gift from the Faculty Senate.

"Cheers," he says to Olive.

"Salud," she says.

As she begins to prepare their dinner he walks out back into his yard. An Elvis tune, so strange, won't get out of his head: *"Is your heart—da da da, will you dum da da da— Tell me—la da da da da . . ."* Oh boy. Elvis.

The blooms on Flo's bush are long gone. Will he plant his little truck garden now that Joe has gone? Well, he may—he won't double its size, that he knows for sure. But maybe he'll add summer squash with the tomatoes and the bush beans. Maybe surprise Olive with a row of okra. She's a Southern gal, likes okra and tomatoes, good slimy stuff. And maybe he will paint the old garage. As for the bees, he will—good God.

He has passed by the first big ash tree and gone under the second one and has looked, from where he stands drink in hand by the edge of the garage at the rear of the yard, up—and sees the bees. Like, wow. Sees the Bees.

There is a tremendous thick, long symmetrical hive in the top of the tree. It is like a great dark cylinder of bee-life. They are absolutely still and quiet, as one, a million bees. They will be going somewhere. Now they are passing through, stopping at his house, their way station, sojourning in this place that has always had, and mostly welcomes, bees. He is glad, so terribly glad, in his heart that they know he was not going to kill them, that he had no interest in poisoning them again. Stanley lifts his Famous Grouse in a salute to them. He passes under them and goes back in.

The next morning he and Olive marvel together that they are still there.

By evening, when Olive and Stanley return from school and shop, the bees have gone. There is, Stanley finds, no remnant left looping around the back of the garage, either.

"In the spring," says Stanley. "In the spring they'll come down the chimney, again. I'm sure we'll have some back here in the spring."

"Oh yes," says Olive. "I have no doubt. I just can't wait."

The last day of October is a fine day. Stanley feels a surge of energy. He decides to teach both his classes, the morning lit class and the afternoon writing class, on campus. Each is in the large seminar room with the round table in his building, his office on the floor just above, which is his university's first building ever built and offered to the bold prairie stretching all around as sign and signification of the enterprise of learning. When the university began a hundred years ago, everything was in this one domed building: Chemistry in the basement by the bookstore, Theology and Theatre and Art and Business (Commerce) up top, History and Literature in the middle and old Dr. Norwick, the first president, for whom Norwick Baine was named, in his office across from Stanley's present seminar room. Stanley has read about Highland U. then, at the beginning of the twentieth century. From what he's read they had fun, then. It must have been a good and happy, energizing, time, then, beginning a university out away from the city where there was nothing. It must have been like a real community.

In the lit class they are winding up Hem and *The Sun Also Rises*. Stanley leads them through the restraint and irony of the ending of the novel, as Jake receives Brett's wire, after his getting-it-back-to-gether and swim in San Sebastian, and takes the Sud Express to Madrid and finds her in the Hotel Montana. The obliqueness of the dialogue is puzzling to these students, as theirs would be to Hem, also the strange little exchange with the short fat woman authority in the hotel. Why would she say the people staying there "were rigidly selectioned"? Was that supposed to be funny? Why does Jake Barnes say he would "welcome the upbringal of my bags"?

"It's not speech, not in quotes," Stanley says. "It is reported on. Indirect discourse, right?"

"She's supposed to be, like, Spanish."

"Are they speaking Spanish?"

"Yeah. But it's like being reported in English."

"I don't see it. The only thing I see here he says in Spanish is 'muy buenos.' So are they talking in Spanish or English or doing a thing on *Saturday Night Live*, ha, you know, 'Un-deep—or Boring—Thoughts'?"

"People communicate formally but, like, artificially, and this gig between Jake boy and the fat lady sets up the artificialness of when Brett and Jake have to talk about, you know, it," says Jim Riddle.

Stanley gives him a nod. Jim has come along.

"It's like in your paper you wrote, you know," Naktasha tells Jim, "it's just *sad*. Man got no—no sexual power, or whatever, woman got a big lady title and social standing, you know, and she's a nympho, and all. It's a symbol of the *age*."

"It's not a symbol," says Margaret, who is an English major. "We should be looking at the subtext of this text."

"It just is *sad*."

"Like my paper talks about," says Jim, getting excited, "it's that the impotent have the job of taking care of everybody and being like guardian angels on the sidelines because they can't, you know, like— do anything direct—"

This wakes up Wild Willy, the boy from Belfast, who happens to be in this class but rarely speaks. He is not as engaged as he was with Q-Man and the others in the writing and the climbing of the mountain at Fort Godwin.

"My Go-ad!" he says. "What's the bloody problem? If they lo-ave each other, don't ride around in a friggin' taxi having an iro-anic time—get with it, I say! Go o'an and have a happy life! There are a dozen ways of making physical lo-ave, y' know, pen-etration or non-pen-etration, even if you can't get it oop!"

"A new reading for our time," Jim Riddle says.

"We'll move on now to Scott Fitzgerald and *The Great Gatsby*," says that great little Stoic teacher Stanley Morris to the class. "If you have read the novel before, please do read it again. Notice the similarity of structure in these two books, both told in the first person by detached"—Dear Lord, he almost says "retinas"—"narrators. They are both what we used to call 'impressionistic' works of art. Go look at some paintings in the Museum of Art downtown or the gallery on campus here. You'll get a sense of what it means. There's a Goya of schoolboys clustered around a table in our gallery that only when you get the right distance back from it . . .”

But, adjusting their caps and the straps of their backpacks on their shoulders, they are out of there, out of Lit and are off to Stat or Chem or Poly Sci or Entrepreneurship or the shift at the Black-eyed Pea or Blimpies or the trek to one of the campus's five specialized libraries, or whatever.

The writing class goes pretty well, too, that afternoon. Stanley has given them a three-paragraph AP story about a mother moose in Anchorage that is harassed by college students throwing snowballs at her and her calf and that kills a seventy-year-old Asian male employee of the college by trampling him one Friday afternoon. On the next Monday, a male professor is running to class and is attacked on the campus path by the “killer moose.” She tries to kick the professor once, then again, but stumbles in the snow. The Alaska Department of Fish and Game decides to kill the moose “because of ‘evidence of ill disposition’” and do so. So, realizing that any story is changed by a shift in point of view and that the key to “reality” (artificial construct as that is) in any story is your choice of point of view, the old “angle of vision,” what POV would you tell this story from?

They scribble away at it, then have a pretty lively discussion.

At the bell Stanley speaks to a couple of students who need to set up conferences with him as the others file out. Then he pauses at the round table, puttering with his stuff, feeling just a wee bit pooped.

He is startled to see the dean—Dean Alice Pendleton Burns herself—looking pretty relaxed and rather lovely, seated in the chair with the writing arm just outside the door to this seminar room. She is reading the handout page of the moose assignment he has stacked there for the students to pick up and read as they entered. She looks up at him and grins.

"The moose win?" she says.

"No. A few liked the moose POV, but were having trouble getting into the moose mentality. It came out kind of, oh, omniscient with sympathy for the mother moose. Smoky the Bear, you know—cartoony."

"That's what I would have done at their age, probably."

"Well, some of them tried the viewpoint of the old Asian guy who had nothing to do with it but is gratuitously killed by this enraged moose trying to protect her calf. And several tried to imagine being one or another of the students throwing snowballs, and why they threw them and tormented the moose, and what they felt about the result, and so on."

"That's nice. I think we have terrific students, don't you? And, see, you teach them values, as in this exercise, all the time. What viewpoint did you choose?"

"The professor, of course. So—" Stanley laughs. "So he can review it and speculate on it and try to make some sense of it. What would you do?"

She stands up, kind of jumps to her feet like the basketball player she was or a head cheerleader. She is wearing a gold-trimmed deep blue silk suit with shoulders like a man's.

"Oh," she says, "as the student of comparative religions I would do an omniscient, or detached, view. I'm afraid it would be like a professional paper, Stanley, if I may call you that. You know, be a professor, just as you said you would do. Look at the meanings of the

moose, its wildness in nature, its encroachment on society, and society's on it, and our need to stone the mother moose and kill her.
Whatever, as the students say. But that wouldn't make much of a
story, would it?"

"No," he says. "It wouldn't."

"So what would really be the best, the most interesting, point of
view, Stanley?"

He smiles at her. She is pretty cool. He starts to call her Alice
but does not, but knows he will eventually.

"Not a detached point of view but more an involved one, of
course. A participant's viewpoint, of someone actually in the story
who cares about the moose, or the old guy, or something . . ."

She waits a second, calibrating him, then says, "Exactly!"

"Whatever," says Stanley. Actually, he is about out of moose.

She smiles again, and whops him on the arm, putting the
handout back on the chair arm.

"OK," she says. "I know it appears I don't have much to do, be-
sides hang out in the hall here and harass teachers, but in fact I am
quite busy. Actually, we are fairly into it, as you may know. Just
noticed on the schedule you were teaching here now, Professor
Morris. So—"

Now her eyes take on a harder, more serious look, but she is still
grinning at him. Her hand that is not affirming her speech is on her
hip.

"So if you will follow me up, my dear sir, do I have a deal for you!
It involves this task force of which you have heard, on human and
academic values in our university. It involves academic and moral
leadership. Your dean is about to name a chair for it."

"I—"

"It really is a hell of a deal, Stanley. Long hours. No extra compensation. A lot of time and thought spent outside your field—but what exactly are our fields these days? I doubt your man Emerson would mind the widening of the boundary."

"Well—"

"Working through some knotty things with some of our toughest and meanest characters who must be put on the committee, who will surely sniff and scratch and bark at each other. Eh?"

"Hell of a deal," Stanley says.

"So, come along then, Morris, if you wish, and we will talk about it, the nitty and the gritty of it."

Her smile beckons. She turns and walks towards the stairs going up to the dean's suite. Watching her go up with a sort of erotic stateliness, watching the movement of the blue and gold, Stanley feels a surge, in his heart, in his loins. Dear Lord.

He follows her.

It will be all right, he tells himself. Olive will understand.

Then Stanley laughs, to himself, following Dean Burns up the stairs.

Oh yes. Olive will understand, all right. You bet she will.

John M. Lewis

MARSHALL TERRY, a former department chair and associate provost at Southern Methodist University, where he has taught for five decades, is the author of seven works of fiction, as well as numerous essays and reviews. He thinks of Stanley Morris as a distillation, like fine aged Scotch, of his own physical and professional experiences. Former president of the Texas Institute of Letters, Terry was honored by that organization in 1991 with the Lon Tinkle Award for "a career of excellence in letters."